Pizza Man

by Darlene Craviotto

A SAMUEL FRENCH ACTING EDITION

SAMUEL FRENCH

FOUNDED 1830

New York Hollywood London Toronto

SAMUELFRENCH.COM

For Richard Seff

PIZZA MAN was first presented by The Slice of Life Company at the Callboard Theatre in Los Angeles, on May 13, 1982. It was produced by Paul Waigner with the following cast:

JULIE RODGERS .... Daphne Eckler
ALICE MEYERLINK .... Wendi Jo Sperber
EDDIE........................... Mark L. Taylor

Standbys: Jude St. James, Louise Hoven, Philip Levien

Directed by Frank Cavestani
Set Design by David Sackeroff
Costumes by Judy Evans
Associate Producer: Carl Sautter
Production Stage Manager: Robert Schanche

PIZZA MAN was subsequently presented by Thursday Night Productions at the Richmond Shepard Theatre in Hollywood, California on April 7, 1983. It was produced by Robert Schanche with the following cast:

JULIE RODGERS .... Kit McDonough
ALICE MEYERLINK .... Kathy Bendett
EDDIE............................ Philip Levien

Standbys: Christine Dickinson, Nancy Cartwright, Rick Dean

Directed by Richard Altman
Production Design by W. Lansing Barbour
Stage Manager: Rick Lucero

ACT ONE

Friday. A long, hot, summer night.

ACT TWO

SCENE ONE

Later that evening.

SCENE TWO

Much later that same evening.

CHARACTER BREAKDOWN

JULIE RODGERS: *Late-twenties. Very attractive. Wholesome. The "girl next door." She's a woman who's lived on her own for a long time and hasn't been successful at it. She's gone through life as a "good girl," a "nice person," and it has led nowhere. She's witty, charming, and intelligent. She's a lady who has style. And she's also a woman who's filled with rage. In the course of the play the rage surfaces.*

ALICE MEYERLINK: *Mid-twenties. Jewish. Constantly battling her weight. Neurotic. This woman doesn't live life ... she attacks it. The smallest event in her day can throw her into the deepest depression or the highest of highs. The real moments in life, however, Alice has a tendency to miss.*

EDDIE (PIZZA MAN): *Late-twenties. Attractive. Cocky. And with a vulnerability he tries desperately to cover up. He likes to think he's macho but on him it really misses. Probably identifies with Burt Reynolds. Eddie is a "nice guy" and he's been paying a price for it his whole life.*

PIZZA MAN

ACT ONE

The house lights dim slowly. We are in black. After a moment a
song begins to play. A hard and sensual Elton John song that
is being played much too loudly. The curtain opens in black
and we see a match being lit. It illuminates the face of a
woman in her late twenties: her very late twenties, who
stands center stage wearing a workshirt and nothing else.
JULIE RODGERS stares into the flame. She has a young
face but we can see the beginnings of lines around her eyes
and mouth. Tight. Cold. Bitter. A face that fluctuates be-
tween "the girl next door" and a woman who has been on
her own for a long time ... and has not been successful at it.
JULIE lights her cigarette, inhales it deeply, pauses, then
blows out the match.

The lights come up slowly onstage to reveal the apartment.
Nothing fancy, it is a simple one bedroom with a small
kitchen nook upstage right. The furniture came with the
apartment and has seen better days. There has been an
attempt, however, at camouflaging most of it with mis-
cellaneous and mismatched throw pillows, slip covers, and
an afghan that is obviously the product of some distant
arthritic aunt. Several pictures on the walls are attractive,
but the majority are simply framed posters purchased at

7

"head shops." They are souvenirs of earlier, more innocent years. The apartment is clean, but cluttered enough to be comfortable. The ashtray on the coffee table is filled with butts. Several empty beer cans are strewn about. JULIE carries one in her hand as she crosses to the TV set. Picking up the TV Guide, she paces the room nervously reading it; moving like a panther in a cage. Dissatisfied with the evening's choices, she tosses it into an armchair, stops and chugalugs the rest of her beer, and then crosses into the kitchen for another. The phone rings loudly. JULIE stops and checks her watch. She nods her head knowingly and crosses to it.

JULIE. *(into phone, matter of factly)* Good evening, Mr. Plotkin. It's 7:45 and you're trying to sleep and you want me to turn down my music, right? *(beat)* I knew it was you, Mr. Plotkin because for the last two years you have called me every night and asked me to turn down my music. And *every night* for the last two years I've turned it down. *(Deep breath. Bravely announcing.)* Tonight ... I'm not turning it down! *(Beat. She listens politely.)* I understand that. *(beat)* I understand you're a senior citizen and you need your sleep. *(her anger mounting)* But the fact is, Mr. Plotkin, you're an old fuck ... *(correcting herself quickly)* ... FART ... *(what the hell)* ... A FUCK FART! *(She slams down the receiver and heads quickly into the kitchen. Suddenly, she stops and thinks a moment; puzzled by her emotional snit with an old man. She mumbles quietly.)* "Fuck fart?" *(Shaking her head, she continues into the kitchen and grabs another beer quickly. Opening it, she takes a long belt and moves back into the living room. Closing her eyes, she lets the music take hold of her. She sways her body sen-*

sually to the hard bass beat of the song.)

(The phone rings.)

JULIE. *(Crosses to it. Into phone.)* Talk quickly, I'm having a nervous breakdown. *(beat)* Look, Mr. Plotkin, give me a break! It's hot. I've had a bad day. It's Friday night and I don't have a date. And I'm not looking forward to spending the evening with my neurotic roommate. Allow me this one hour in my own apartment to go berserk! *(beat)* Doing? *(beat)* I'm not doing anything. *(beat)* I *am not* dancing naked in my apartment! *(Picking up the phone and moving to the window. Shouting at him through it.)* And what the *HELL* are you doing looking in my window?!!! *(beat)* The curtains are closed. They're thin curtains. *(beat)* I won't put underwear on. I have underwear on. *(beat)* I do. *(beat)* I do. I do, GODDAMNIT, I DO!!! *(Her back to the audience, she rips open her workshirt, exposing herself in front of the window. A beat. She looks down and discovers to her horror that she is in fact naked.)* Oh my God. *(picking up the phone quickly)* I'm sorry, Mr. Plotkin. I could have sworn I had underwear on. *(beat)* Hello? ... Mr. Plotkin? Hello? ... Oh God. *(She hangs up quickly. Stands a moment looking totally lost and embarrassed. She hugs the shirt tightly to her body and hurries toward the bedroom to put on some clothes.)*

(The front door suddenly bursts open and the neurotic roommate enters. ALICE MEYERLINK is in her mid-twenties. She is a woman who does not live life ... she attacks it. The smallest event in her day can throw her into the deepest depression or the highest of highs. This includes breaking a fingernail, missing a bus, getting a

FUCK PART

date, not getting a date, etc., etc. The real moments in her life however, ALICE has a tendency to miss. ALICE's entrance is a dramatic one. She slams the front door behind her and leans against it wearily. The phone rings again.)

JULIE. *(as she enters into the bedroom)* Alice, could you get the phone? *(JULIE disappears into the bedroom. ALICE remains frozen in front of the door. The phone continues to ring persistantly. JULIE calls from offstage.)* Alice, the phone! *(ALICE remains frozen. The phone rings on. JULIE calls from offstage.)* Could you get the damn phone!!! *(ALICE moves over to a poster of Mexico hanging on the wall. She rips it down furiously. She moves to a nearby table. She snatches silk flowers from a porcelain vase. She starts to turn away, hesitates, and then turns back and picks up the vase too. She carries all of these things to a nearby wastebasket. And she victoriously drops them inside of it. Without hesitating she moves over to a large bulletin board up on the wall. She rips down the following items: a large Hallmark Valentine's card with a huge heart on it, four Polaroid snapshots, and a L.A. Kings banner. She tosses these also into the wastebasket. ALICE heads into the bedroom, passing JULIE on her way out of the bedroom.)* Why didn't you answer the phone? *(ALICE ignores her and disappears into the bedroom.)* Alice? *(JULIE rushes over to the phone, picking it up...)* Hello? *(to herself)* Oh God. *(sweetly)* Hello, Mother? How are you?

(Offstage, drawers open and slam loudly.)

JULIE. No, I'm fine, Mom. I was in the bedroom changing.

(Offstage the drawers continue to slam. JULIE starts to get up and head into the bedroom to see what's happening.)

JULIE. *(bored)* No, I'm not going out tonight. Is that why you called?

(As JULIE heads towards the bedroom a jewelry box comes flying out of the bedroom door. JULIE reacts.)

JULIE. I know it's Friday night, Mother. And it's a "convenient" night to go out ... But I just want to spend a nice quiet evening at home.

(Several articles of clothing are thrown out from the bedroom and also a pink plastic vibrator.)

JULIE. Who? ... Mary Jo Sweeny ... Yeah? *(JULIE picks up the vibrator and looks at it.)* Yeah. I went to high school with her ... Why? *(JULIE sits slowly in the armchair. Beat. She is used to having these kinds of conversations with her mother and speaks habitually now.)* When did she die, Mom? *(beat)* What did she die from? *(quickly)* Mother, she had that in high school. She was a very sick girl.

(ALICE struggles out of the bedroom carrying a portable trampoline. With great difficulty she carries it to the front door and exits.)

JULIE. Of course I'm sorry she died. I'm very sorry. Mary Jo Sweeny was a very sweet girl. But why do you have to call me every time a school mate of mine dies? I

you see a school mate of mine

hate these tragic late breaking bulletins. *(beat)* I realize
life is short and we have to go out and live it. But, Mom
I'm only staying home this *one Friday night!*

*(ALICE enters the apartment and heads over to the couch. She
collapses exhaustedly on top of it.)*

JULIE. Mother, I can't deal with this right now. I have
to go. Sarah Bernhardt just came home. *(She hangs up the
phone. She stares at ALICE for a long moment.)* Please. Nothing
dramatic.

ALICE. I don't want to live.

JULIE. Should I sit down for this?

ALICE. *(dramatically)* A woman puts her whole heart
and soul into a relationship. And what does it get
her?

JULIE. I hate to ask.

ALICE. A pocketful of heartaches!

JULIE. A pocketful of heartaches.

ALICE. I did everything for that man. I gave him my
life for thirteen months. I went to stupid hockey games
with him. I went to cheap and sordid motels. I lost weight
for him! And how does he repay me? (BEAT)

JULIE. I give up.

ALICE. *(the grand declaration)* He went back to his
wife!

JULIE. Oh brother.

ALICE. Is there anything to eat? *(She heads quickly for
the kitchen.)* Alice In kitchen

JULIE. Hold it. Wait a minute. Did you have
dinner?

ALICE. Twice.   *What are you doing?*

JULIE. *(Stops her.)* I'm not going to let you do this to
yourself. You've lost 25 pounds in four months and I'm
not going to watch you gain it back in one night.

ALICE. But I'm depressed!

JULIE. You always eat when you get depressed and
then you get depressed because you ate. And then you
eat again. Within a month you'll be back in queen
size pantyhose.

ALICE. At least I'm not an alcoholic!

JULIE. Don't attack me because you're upset.

ALICE. *(noticing a beer in JULIE's hand)* That isn't apple
juice, is it?

JULIE. *(defensively)* It's a before dinner drink.

ALICE. You smell like you've had at least four
dinners.   *How many dinners did you have?*

JULIE. We were supposed to eat an hour ago. I'm not
going to eat alone.

ALICE. Why not? You drink alone.

JULIE. Look, don't start. It was very pleasant before
you came home.

ALICE. Fine! Maybe I'll leave!

JULIE. Fine. Leave!   *Face to Face*

ALICE. Fine. I will!

JULIE. Fine. Go!

ALICE. OK. FINE! *(ALICE exits quickly, slamming the door
loudly after her. JULIE takes a long swallow of beer, crosses to the
couch, takes a beat, and then crosses up to the front door. She opens*   *(BEAT)*
*it slowly. ALICE stands in the doorway sheepishly. The two women
look at each other. Automatically...)*

JULIE / ALICE. *(flatly)* I'm sorry.

ALICE. *(enters)* I'm so depressed. He went back to his wife! Do you believe that?! He's been telling me for over a year how much he loves me and then he goes back to his wife! I hope he has a stroke, the sonofabitch. Jerry went back to his wife!!!

~~JULIE. I heard.~~

ALICE. *(quickly)* ~~Who'd you hear it from?~~ *(hopefully)* ~~Did he call?~~ Did he call me?

~~JULIE. You. You just told me!~~   No

ALICE. I don't know what I'm saying. I'm so depressed. I have to eat. I can't cope with this. *(She goes into the kitchen.)* Alice to kitchen / Julie sits.

JULIE. *(Sits down on the couch slowly. ~~Looking up at the heavens.)~~* Not tonight. Please. I won't make it through the night.

ALICE. *(screaming from the kitchen)* THERE'S NOTHING TO EAT IN HERE!!! *(Hurries back into the living room.)* What happened to all the food? You were supposed to go to the store today.

JULIE. *(uninterested)* I was?

ALICE. I gave you my twenty dollars this morning. You made a big deal about it. You said you wanted to do the shopping because I always buy diet food.

~~JULIE. I did?~~

~~ALICE. You said that if you ever saw another rye crisp again you'd beat it to a pulp.~~

~~JULIE. I forgot.~~

ALICE. *(incredulously)* You forgot to go shopping?

~~JULIE. I guess.~~

ALICE. Terrific. *(She paces.)* I *need* food! I can't suffer on an empty stomach!

JULIE. Have a beer.

ALICE. *(beat)* Beer?

JULIE. Or wine. There's some Spanada in the refrigerator.

ALICE. *(Rushes into the kitchen. She returns carrying a six pack of beer, a bottle of wine, and a quart of scotch. Slowly.)* Are we having a party tonight?

JULIE. I'm not.

ALICE. Why do we have all this? *(JULIE shrugs. Suspiciously.)* Where's my twenty dollars?

JULIE. Did you give me twenty dollars?

ALICE. Did you spend my twenty dollars on this?

JULIE. I think so.

ALICE. What's that mean?

JULIE. Yes! Yes I did!

ALICE. *(pause)* Are you drunk?

JULIE. I'm getting there.

ALICE. Wonderful! My whole world explodes in my face and the one night I need someone to lean on ... to tell my troubles to and you decide to fall apart!

JULIE. *(quickly)* I'm not falling apart.

ALICE. Whatever.

JULIE. I'm not falling apart!!!

ALICE. *(Pause. Stares at JULIE. Quietly.)* OK. OK.

JULIE. *(beat)* And what do you mean the *one* night you need me to tell your troubles to? What the hell do we do here seven nights a week? I'm beginning to feel like Ann Landers. God help me if I ever have a problem and need your help.

ALICE. You're the most together person I know. You never have problems. It's disgusting.

JULIE. That's what you think.

ALICE. You do have problems?

JULIE. Of course I have problems.

ALICE. That's wonderful.

JULIE. What?

ALICE. I was beginning to wonder. You never yell. You never get upset. Whenever anything goes wrong you just sit there and smile. It's infuriating. You've got perfect teeth.

JULIE. Just because I don't run around telling the world I've got problems doesn't mean I don't have problems. I have problems.

ALICE. *(sweetly)* Do we have a little problem tonight?

JULIE. Don't talk to me like that.

ALICE. Like what?

JULIE. Like I'm on Romper Room and I just wet my pants.

ALICE. I'm *sorry.* Excuse *me* ... I just want you to know if you have a problem I'm here to listen.

JULIE. *(Beat. Softly.)* I do. I do have a problem.

ALICE. Oh thank you. I need that tonight. I need to feel needed. I really need it ...

JULIE. *(interrupting)* Can I get on with my problem?

ALICE. Sure. You wanna lie down on the couch? *(rising)* Let me get some paper. I'll take notes.

JULIE. Forget it.

ALICE. I want to listen.

JULIE. Just forget it!

ALICE. I'll listen.

JULIE. *FOR-GET IT!!!*

ALICE. *(Silence. Softly.)* Please, Julie?

JULIE. *(Pause. Quietly.)* I yelled at Mr. Plotkin tonight.

ALICE. Old Mr. Plotkin with the hearing aid? I always yell at him. He can't hear.

JULIE. No, I mean I really yelled at him. He called up about the music and I ... *(beat)* ... I called him an old fuck fart.

ALICE. *(shocked)* My God!

JULIE. I don't even know what a fuck fart is.

ALICE. *(laughing)* That's great. I like that. Old fuck fart Plotkin. I always wanted to call him something like that. *(Stops laughing. Suddenly serious.)* I was always afraid he'd have a stroke or something.

JULIE. I took off my shirt and exposed myself.

ALICE. For Plotkin?

JULIE. Yeah.

ALICE. What'd he do?

JULIE. I think he had a stroke. I'm not sure. I thought I heard him breathing but I'm not sure.

ALICE. He'll get over it.

JULIE. I yelled at people at work. Driving home I yelled at people on the road. Then you came home and I yelled at you.

ALICE. Julie, that's not like you.

JULIE. *(yelling)* I know it's not like me! God, I'm doing it again.

ALICE. Is there a reason for all this? All this yelling?

JULIE. I'm uptight, that's all. I'm just uptight.

ALICE. My mother has always said when a woman gets like this it's because she hasn't slept well, eaten well, or exercised. *Now,* you went to bed early last night so that's not it. When's the last time you exercised?

JULIE. This morning.

ALICE. We'll order a pizza. *(She moves quickly to the phone.)*

JULIE. I'm not hungry.

ALICE. *(desperately)* Well I am! There's nothing to eat in this house!!!

JULIE. *(topping her)* I LOST MY JOB!!! *(Silence. Quietly.)* They laid me off.

ALICE. Oh Julie. You were doing so well. You were there almost five months.

JULIE. Six.

ALICE. What happened?

JULIE. I don't know. I'm not sure. Last week my boss called me into his office. I thought he was gonna dictate a letter. He said sit down. I said thank you. He said you're a good secretary. I said thank you. He said you're very pretty. I said thank you. He said you wanna go out for a drink later? I said no thank you. And today I got a pink slip with my check.

ALICE. He wouldn't.

JULIE. He did.

ALICE. He can't.

JULIE. He did. Business is bad. He's laying people off. I wouldn't lay him. So he's laying me off. It all sounds so poetic.

ALICE. *(angrily)* That's unethical! He could get into a lot of trouble doing this!

JULIE. *(flatly)* Yeah, his wife would kill him if she knew. She's a large woman.

ALICE. We should call somebody and report this! ... Eyewitness News!!!

~~JULIE. Call his wife. She's large. Really large. A huge woman.~~

ALICE. *(interrupting)* How can you be so calm about all this? No wonder you're uptight. You should fight this!

~~JULIE. It's not the first job I've lost. I'll go back to unemployment.~~

ALICE. God, this makes me so angry! *(paces dramatically)*

~~JULIE. *(surprised)* It does?~~

ALICE. I'm furious! Can't you tell? I'm furious! *(still pacing angrily)*

~~JULIE. That's sweet, Alice. I didn't expect that from you. Getting so involved in my problems you could forget your own.~~

ALICE. *(passionately)* You want to know what would have happened if you had that drink with him? One drink would've led to six drinks would've led to ten. And before you know it ... *(snaps fingers)* ... just like that it'd be a year later and he would've gone back to his wife! Just like Jerry. *(beat)* Don't we at least have some celery? *(She heads for the kitchen.)* Just a stalk of celery. Something to chew on...   (BEAT)

~~JULIE. *(Checks her watch.)* Two minutes. Two minutes on my problem.~~

JULIE. *(Heads into the kitchen as ALICE frantically searches the refrigerator.)* I ~~MAY NOT BE ABLE TO PAY THE RENT!~~

ALICE. I thought we had peanut butter. I could've sworn there was peanut butter.

JULIE. *(stopping ALICE)* Look at me. Read my lips. *(speaking to a deaf person) Money!* I may not have any. I'm talking about practical things. Real life. Stop thinking about this schmuck.

ALICE. He's not a schmuck.

JULIE. He's a married man. He's a schmuck!

ALICE. You're just saying that because you got burned once.

JULIE. All right, so didn't you learn anything from that? Didn't you learn from my affair with Allen?

ALICE. You never gave poor Allen a chance.

JULIE. What do you mean I didn't give him a chance?

ALICE. You dropped him when you found out he was married.

JULIE. Of course I dropped him. I did the right and proper thing.

ALICE. Well, if you're going to do the right and proper thing you'll be single the rest of your life.

JULIE. So what was I supposed to do? Keep seeing him? Wait him out?

ALICE. No. Never. Allen was a shit.

JULIE. *(suddenly defensive)* Allen was a wonderful man. He was intelligent, sensitive. Good looking...

ALICE. But he wore Brooks Brothers suits.

JULIE. What does that mean?

ALICE. A man in a Brooks Brothers suit can never be trusted.

JULIE. You're kidding, right? Please tell me you're kidding.

ALICE. C'mon, Julie. Didn't your mother ever talk to you?

JULIE. My mother barely told me about menstruation. She gave me a booklet she sent away for from the Kotex corporation. She's not the type of woman who would give me a list of rules and regulations for illicit love affairs.

ALICE. All right, look. Pay attention. If a woman is going to have a successful love affair with a married man it's got to be with a guy like Jerry. He's balding. He's not the brightest. Doesn't make that much money. Wears suits from Zachary All. He's not too good in bed. And he's short.

JULIE. Why would you want to marry a man like that?

ALICE. Because I honestly feel he'd never cheat on me.

JULIE. He's already cheating on his wife!

ALICE. All right, once. He's a young man. He's getting it out of his system.

JULIE. (Just stares at ALICE in disbelief.) Why are you here, Alice? Why are you in my life? You never listen to me. You ask me for advice but you never listen. (getting angry) It's like talking to a goddamn wall! I'm trying to communicate with a goddamn raving idiot! You're an IDIOT, Alice! An I.D.I.O.T. ... IDIOT!!!

ALICE. (smiles) I know what you're doing. And I appreciate it.

JULIE. Pardon?

ALICE. You're yelling at me because you care.

JULIE. I do?

ALICE. You're wonderful, Julie. Really wonderful.

JULIE. I am?

ALICE. We're not just roommates.

JULIE. We're not?

ALICE. You know what we are?

JULIE. What?

ALICE. We're sisters.

JULIE. Oh God.

ALICE. Buddies!

JULIE. Buddies?

ALICE. I never had a buddy.

JULIE. Really? *sister*

ALICE. Never had a buddy. Never.

JULIE. Gee. *oh God*

ALICE. I'd do anything for you.

JULIE. You would?

ALICE. Anything. Would you do anything for me?

JULIE. Well ...

ALICE. *(quickly)* I'd do anything for *you.*

JULIE. ... Yes.

ALICE. Anything?

JULIE. Sure.

ALICE. *(desperate)* Julie, please. Let me have a piece of your bread. *(BEAT)*

JULIE. I can't do that.

ALICE. Please tell me where you hide your bread.

JULIE. I promised you when you moved in I'd never tell you where I hide my fattening foods.

ALICE. One piece. One little piece.

JULIE. You know you won't stop after one piece.

ALICE. I will. I promise.

JULIE. You won't

ALICE. I will.

JULIE. You won't

ALICE. *(grabbing JULIE)* Tell me where you hide your goddamn bread!!!

JULIE. *(quickly)* The bedroom. Top drawer of the dresser. *(ALICE races into the bedroom.)*

(Much slamming and banging offstage.) (NOISE)

ALICE. *(Rushes back into the living room with an empty plastic wrapper.)* It's gone! It's all gone!

JULIE. I finished it this morning.

ALICE. I HATE YOU!!! *(Rushes to a closet near the front door. She pulls out a suitcase and several of her coats.)*

JULIE. What're you doing?

ALICE. Moving out! *(She begins packing.)*

JULIE. Alice.

ALICE. Don't try to stop me. I knew this would never work! A size 7 rooming with a size 10.

JULIE. Relax. Sit down.

ALICE. God save me from Goyim!

JULIE. You're not making any sense. Sit down...

ALICE. This place is a dump. You don't even have shag rugs!

JULIE. *(stopping her)* SIT!!! *(ALICE sits. JULIE sits next to her.)* Now, just relax. We'll relax. Forget about what's happened to us today.

ALICE. *(pause)* I can only think of Jerry.

JULIE. *(She gives up.)* We'll watch television. *(She heads for the set.)*

ALICE. *(loudly)* I hate television! All those commercials.

FOOD commercials. Jack in the Box. Sarah Lee. Jeno's Pizza... I want a pizza! *(Rises quickly and heads for the door.)*

JULIE. *(Stops her.)* You're not going out for pizza.

ALICE. *(hopefully)* We could call Pizza Man. He delivers.

JULIE. NO! You're not gonna use food to get through this evening. We'll put on the stereo and listen to music. *(Heads over to the stereo.)*

ALICE. I hate music! It's depressing. All those love songs.

JULIE. Isn't there anything that doesn't depress you?

ALICE. Only food. And you won't let me have any. You're very cruel, Julie.

JULIE. You'll thank me for it tomorrow.

ALICE. I may not be around tomorrow. I may die in my sleep of a bleeding ulcer. It's not good to be emotional on an empty stomach.

JULIE. It's not empty. You had dinner. TWICE!

ALICE. That was an hour ago. I digest quickly when I'm upset. *(Paces the room anxiously.)* I feel so frustrated! If I could just laugh or cry. Anything! Just to let the pain out... *(moving to phone)* I'll call Jerry. I always feel better when I talk to Jerry...

JULIE. *(Follows her.)* Forget Jerry. You don't need Jerry.

ALICE. Yes, I do! I really do.

JULIE. Make yourself feel better. C'mon. Try laughing.

ALICE. It's not funny. *(Starts to dial.)*

JULIE. *(Takes the phone away from her.)* Years from now you'll look back at this and laugh. You'll think of all the crazy things you did for him and you won't even remember his name.

ALICE. *(Flatly attempts a laugh.)* Ha.

JULIE. That's it. Come on.

ALICE. Ha. Ha.

JULIE. Good. Very good.

ALICE. *(flatly)* Ha. Ha. Ha. Ha. Ha. Ha. Ha. Ha. Ha. *(beat)* Maybe crying would help.

JULIE. He's not worth crying over.

ALICE. I know. But it makes me feel better. Don't you feel better after a good cry? *(pause)* I say don't you feel better after you've cried? *(JULIE shrugs.)* What does that mean?

JULIE. *(quietly)* I can't cry.

ALICE. What do you mean you can't cry?

JULIE. I *can't* cry.

ALICE. Everybody cries.

JULIE. I can't.

ALICE. Of course you can.

JULIE. No, I can't.

ALICE. Really?

JULIE. Yes.

ALICE. Never?

JULIE. Well. *(beat)* I used to cry all the time when I was younger. But not anymore.

ALICE. Maybe you've got a blocked tear duct.

JULIE. Pardon?

ALICE. When your tear ducts get blocked you can't cry.

JULIE. I have perfect tear ducts.

ALICE. Have you had them checked?

JULIE. They're perfect.

ALICE. When's the last time you cried?

JULIE. *(Thinks for a moment.)* Seven years ago.

ALICE. My God. It's been that long? *(JULIE nods.)* What happened seven years ago?

JULIE. It's not important.

ALICE. Of course it's important! It made you cry seven years ago and you haven't cried since? It must have been very important. Maybe if you can remember what it was you can cry again. It's not healthy to walk around with all that liquid inside of you. Now, where were you seven years ago when you did this crying?

JULIE. In an office.

ALICE. Good. That's good. It's a beginning. What kind of office?

JULIE. Wood panelled.

ALICE. Who's office was it? A doctor's? Was that when your tear ducts were checked?

JULIE. My tear ducts are fine.

ALICE. He told you your tear ducts were fine. *That's* when you started crying.

JULIE. He wasn't a doctor.

ALICE. What was he doing in a doctor's office?

JULIE. It wasn't a doctor's office.

ALICE. *(quickly)* A dentist! You went to see a dentist. He pulled a tooth and you cried.

JULIE. This isn't "What's My Line"! I was in a lawyer's office, all right?

ALICE. A wood panelled lawyer's office. Had you been in an accident?

JULIE. No.

ALICE. What kind of lawyer was it?

JULIE. A divorce lawyer.

ALICE. Who was getting a divorce?

JULIE. I was.

ALICE. *(beat)* I didn't hear you.

JULIE. I was!

ALICE. *(Glares at JULIE, quietly angry.)* You never told me you were married.

JULIE. I'm sorry.

ALICE. *(indignant)* I have been living here for eight months and you never mentioned it!

JULIE. I didn't think it was important.

ALICE. *Jerry* didn't think it was important either! And look where he is! I suppose you'll be going back too!!!

JULIE. Back?

ALICE. Well, go ahead. I don't care. I can live alone. I don't need any of you.

JULIE. Alice. You're not well.

ALICE. Jerry goes back to his wife. And you go back to your husband. And Alice will live alone. Fighting Cellulite!

JULIE. I'm not going back to my husband. We're divorced. It was seven years ago.

ALICE. You're just saying that to make me feel better.

JULIE. I promise you. I'm not going back.

ALICE. *(hopefully)* Was it that awful?

JULIE. It had its moments.

ALICE. What happened? Did you stop loving each other?

JULIE. No. I think I still love him.

ALICE. How long were you married?

JULIE. Three months.

ALICE. Three months?! I've had colds that lasted longer than three months.

JULIE. We knew each other since we were kids. We dated all through high school. All four years. We just knew someday we'd get married. We waited until we finished our first year of college just to be sure. *(She smiles a little.)* It was a very long year. I couldn't wait until it was over. We got engaged in June. Got married in the Fall. Got a little apartment on campus and settled in. We couldn't afford to put the two of us through college so I quit and got a job. Ronnie was studying to be a doctor and I figured Medicine was more important than my Liberal Arts Major. I wasn't sure what I wanted to be and it didn't matter anymore. I was married.

ALICE. You gave up a doctor? My God! Why?

JULIE. I came home one afternoon to have lunch with him. It was his birthday and I wanted to surprise him. *(beat)* I found him in bed with my best friend.

ALICE. *(Gasps dramatically.)* Oh no!

JULIE. Oh yes.

ALICE. My God no!

JULIE. Yeah.

ALICE. She couldn't have been such a good friend to do something like that.

JULIE. My best friend. He was like a brother to me.

ALICE. He? You found your husband in bed with a he?!

JULIE. You got it.

ALICE. *(shrugs)* Well, that's nothing.

JULIE. Pardon?

ALICE. It could have been another woman.

JULIE. You think there's nothing wrong with that?

ALICE. He didn't reject you for another woman. And it wasn't just any guy. It was your best friend.

JULIE. I can't talk to you. We just can't talk.

ALICE. Is that the only reason you divorced him?

JULIE. I shouldn't have brought it up.

ALICE. You let a good doctor slip out of your hands because of that?

JULIE. He was gay!

ALICE. One afternoon. One mad, impulsive afternoon. It was his birthday!

JULIE. It had been going on for months.

ALICE. *(calmly)* But Julie, the man was going to be a doctor.

JULIE. What does that mean?

ALICE. Money! Doctors make a lot of money. He's probably got a very wealthy practice by now. And he's blowing the whole wad at gay bars.

JULIE. Bad choice of words.

ALICE. I realize that. *(beat)* Don't you see if you'd hung in you'd probably have a well furnished home in the suburbs, a Mercedes station wagon, great clothes, *maybe* some children, and you wouldn't be sitting here tonight worrying about finding another job.

JULIE. *If* he had become a doctor.

ALICE. He didn't become a doctor?

JULIE. He flunked out of Medical School.

ALICE. What'd he become?

JULIE. A male nurse.

ALICE. Oh that's disgusting! That's really disgusting. A fagelah male nurse. Doesn't he have any originality? You're lucky to be rid of him.

JULIE. Yeah. But it's made things awful tough. I just don't trust men anymore.

ALICE. I know what you mean. Jerry made me all sorts of promises. He loved me. He wanted to marry me. We were going to Yucatan to teach the natives.

JULIE. Yucatan?

ALICE. It's a very backward area.

JULIE. And you believed him?

ALICE. Why not? It was always his dream. He even taught me Spanish.

JULIE. He's a CPA in Encino!

ALICE. So. CPA's can have dreams!

JULIE. Alice. It was a fantasy. And you got mixed up in it. You got burned. Just accept it.

ALICE. *(Thinks a moment. Pouting.)* Well, it seemed like a good idea to me. I don't know. *(beat)* I'll never trust another man as long as I live. *(Looks at JULIE.)* Would you like to turn lesbian with me?

JULIE. No!

ALICE. We could never get pregnant but if we wanted a baby we could buy one in Yucatan. They do that a lot there and I speak the language. *(JULIE stares at ALICE.)* We don't have to have children. We can live alone.

JULIE. *(Heads into the kitchen.)* You want some scotch?

ALICE. No. *(Follows JULIE into the kitchen.)* So if you give up on men but you won't turn gay what else is there? How do you cope?

JULIE. *(Pours herself a scotch.)* I'm doing fine thank you.

ALICE. Sure. You drink. You haven't cried in seven years. And you yell at old men on phones.

JULIE. Today's an off day. *Usually* I do fine.

ALICE. How?

JULIE. I get numb. I wander through supermarkets and life like a zombie. Never getting upset. Never getting angry ... I did go shopping today. But I had to leave. I stood in the jams and jellies for fifteen minutes. Fifteen minutes, Alice. I couldn't decide ... Mint Jelly or Orange Marmalade. I didn't know what I wanted ... And for the first time in my life it pissed me off. *(She takes a drink.)* ... I wanted to smash every jar on the shelf. Run through every aisle and knock everything to the floor. I wanted to explode! ... But, I didn't. I was a good girl. I went home and started drinking. *(She sips at her drink.)* And I will continue to drink. Until the zombie returns. Until everything gets numb again.

ALICE. But drinking isn't good for you, Julie. You should take up eating. I would have bought both of those jams.

JULIE. We shouldn't have to go through any of this. Me getting drunk. You getting fat. It's misplaced anger. And we should just let it out. It's a lot healthier.

ALICE. And cheaper.

JULIE. You know what our problem is? We're not men. Men can be angry anytime they want. Nobody cares. But if a woman even raises her voice she's a bitch. A cunt.

ALICE. *(nods)* A real ballbuster.

JULIE. It's all right for a man to be angry. He can be aggressive and let it out. Get into a fight. Smash in somebody's face. There's always athletics ... You wanna run around the block?

ALICE. I'd never make it.

JULIE. What about tennis?

ALICE. I don't play tennis.

JULIE. Don't you do anything physical?

ALICE. I did. But Jerry's gone back to his wife so that's out. *(She flops down on the couch.)* Maybe I'll kill myself. That's aggressive.

JULIE. Don't be stupid. I'll teach you tennis.

ALICE. *(beat)* Maybe you're right. Maybe I *would* feel better if I could just hit something. Or throw something. *(JULIE hands ALICE a beer can.)* No thanks. Beer makes me hungry.

JULIE. Throw it. *(Hand beer can)*

ALICE. What?

JULIE. Go ahead. Throw it.

ALICE. You mean just throw it?

JULIE. It'll help.

ALICE. *(Takes the can from JULIE.)* Where should I throw it?

JULIE. Throw it anywhere. Don't think about it. *(ALICE stands and looks around. She moves into the kitchen and throws the can into the trash.)* You were supposed to throw it, not throw it away!

ALICE. I don't wanna mess up the apartment. Tomorrow's my turn to clean up.

JULIE. Fuck the apartment! *(She throws ALICE another can.)* Throw it! *(ALICE half-heartedly throws it into a kitchen corner. JULIE throws her another.)*

ALICE. Again?

JULIE. Again.

ALICE. Julie.

JULIE. Throw it!! *(ALICE throws it quickly but automatically into another corner. JULIE immediately throws her another. ALICE throws it automatically. JULIE throws her another. ALICE, like a machine, throws it. JULIE throws ALICE a glass.)*

ALICE. *(She pauses.)* It'll break.

JULIE. Throw it!

ALICE. Julie, it's glass.

JULIE. Throw it!! *(ALICE lightly throws it on the rug. It does not break. JULIE grabs a large ashtray and crosses to ALICE.)* Harder. Come on. Really throw it.

ALICE. *(Throws it a bit harder and the large porcelain ashtray breaks. Quickly.)* OK. That's it. I feel better.

JULIE. *(Hands her another glass.)* Come on, get it out! Really throw it!

ALICE. No, really. I feel better.

JULIE. Throw it!

ALICE. I'm fine now.

JULIE. GODAMNITT!! THROW IT!! *(JULIE hurls the glass into the kitchen and it shatters. It hasn't had time to settle before she reaches for another object and hurls it into the kitchen. Followed by another. And another.)*

ALICE. Julie! *(JULIE continues to throw objects angrily against the kitchen wall.)* My God Julie! *(JULIE picks up the half-filled Spanada jug and hurls it against the wall. It shatters across the kitchen.)* JULIE!!! *(ALICE grabs JULIE. Stopping her. Silence.)* Are you all right? *(JULIE moves away from ALICE and crosses to the couch. Slowly she sits. ALICE is looking around.)* My God. Look at this mess.

JULIE. *(softly)* I don't feel any better.

ALICE. I feel awful. I gotta clean up tomorrow. *(Gets

*down on her hands and knees and starts to pick up the broken pieces
of ashtray.)*

JULIE. *(dazed)* It didn't help.

ALICE. I'm gonna cut myself, I know it.

JULIE. Do you think this is sexual tension?

ALICE. I don't know what the hell it is but it's killing
me. Look at this, I'm bleeding already. *(Sucks her
finger.)*

JULIE. Maybe I should just go out and get picked
up.

ALICE. *(Heads into the kitchen to straighten up.)* That won't
help. All you'll do is lay there.

JULIE. *(correcting her English)* Lie.

ALICE. No, it's the truth. Women just lay there. That's
not aggressive.

JULIE. *(enthusiastically)* You know what I'd do tonight if
I were a man?

ALICE. You're not a man. You're a woman. That's the
whole problem.

JULIE. I'd go out ...

ALICE. *(Moves out of the kitchen.)* I'm not cleaning that up
by myself.

JULIE. ... I'd go to a bar.

ALICE. *(bored)* You'd go out to a bar.

JULIE. And I'd get drunk.

ALICE. You're doing that already.

JULIE. I'd pick up a girl ...

ALICE. Yeah.

JULIE. Any girl ...

ALICE. Yeah.

JULIE. *(beat)* And I'd rape her.

ALICE. *(Stares at JULIE.)* Yes. That would be aggressive. That would be very aggressive. *Sick* but aggressive. *(JULIE turns and looks at ALICE. ALICE continues, nervously.)* We already agreed not to go gay.

JULIE. We don't do it to a girl. We do it to a guy.

ALICE. Oh. *(beat)* You mean rape a guy? *(JULIE smiles.)* We can't do that. Women can't do that.

JULIE. Why not? *(slowly)* Why can't we do it? *(She rises quickly.)* Where's your phone book?

ALICE. What?

JULIE. That little black book with all the phone numbers in it.

ALICE. What're you gonna do?

JULIE. Call a guy and get him over here.

ALICE. And then what?

JULIE. *(smiles)* A little wine. A little music. *(beat)* And then we jump on him! He won't be able to walk when we get through with him.

ALICE. *We're* going to do this?

JULIE. Yes.

ALICE. You and me?

JULIE. *Yes.*

ALICE. *(Roars laughter.)* It'll never work.

JULIE. We can try!

ALICE. I don't do too well just laying there...

JULIE. *(correcting her English) Lying.*

ALICE. No, honest. Now you want me to be an active participant? I've only seen one porno movie in my life.

JULIE. I'm not so innocent. I was married you know.

ALICE. Three months. And he was gay.

JULIE. Between the two of us we'll do fine. Where's your phone book?

ALICE. Why does it have to be one of my friends? I don't want to do this to somebody who might know my mother.

JULIE. You want to do it with a stranger?

ALICE. Absolutely. Ships in the night.

JULIE. Really?

ALICE. Please.

JULIE. All right.

ALICE. *(Picks up the phone and dials "0". Into phone.)* Could I have a listing for Pizza Man?

JULIE. *(Slams her hand down on the phone.)* That's not funny!

ALICE. Julie, I feel faint. Let me have a pizza.

JULIE. No.

ALICE. One piece. I won't eat the crust.

JULIE. NO!

ALICE. Julie, sex is humiliating enough. Please don't make me go through this on an almost empty stomach.

JULIE. *(angrily)* If you get a pizza will you shut up about eating? Will you shut up and can we get on with the evening?

ALICE. *(quickly)* I promise. I'll do anything you want. You can have my phone book. You don't even have to give it back. You could just keep it.

JULIE. All right, call Pizza Man! *(ALICE grabs the phone desperately. Searches the Yellow Pages.. Rips out a page and dials hurriedly. JULIE goes into the kitchen for more scotch.)*

ALICE. *(quickly into phone)* I want the big one. Double

cheese. Double anchovies. Hold the onions. 6555 Lexington Avenue. Apartment 30. And hurry. I'm a big tip-
per. *(ALICE hangs up and sighs deeply. JULIE moves into the
living room. She has a fresh drink in her hand.)* Not that I'm
counting but don't you think you've had enough.

JULIE. Not yet. I still remember who I am.

ALICE. You'll get another job, Julie. Don't worry about
it.

JULIE. Sure, I will. I always do. But I hate the kind of
jobs I end up getting.

ALICE. I can check at work and see if there's an
opening.

JULIE. I don't want to work in the secretarial pool at
Occidental Life.

ALICE. It's not so bad. You get great insurance
coverage.

JULIE. I'm tired of jobs that don't lead anywhere.
Three months waitressing at Dennys. Four months sell-
ing hand bags at the May Company. Three weeks as a
tour guide at the Liberace Mansion.

ALICE. Now that sounds fun.

JULIE. I almost lasted a year at the Hungarian pen
factory.

ALICE. You worked at a Hungarian pen factory?

JULIE. I was a receptionist. We sold pens over the
phone.

ALICE. To Hungarians?

JULIE. No, not Hungarians. To anybody.

ALICE. Were they Hungarian pens?

JULIE. They were made in Japan.

ALICE. You sold Japanese pens in a Hungarian pen

factory?

JULIE. God, I hated that job.

ALICE. I'm not sure I understand this job.

JULIE. The salesmen were all pigs. My boss was a pig. He used to come over and sit on top of my desk. Just sit there and peer down my blouse. Two feet away from the coffee machine and he'd ask me to get up and fix him a coffee. I'd say to him ...

ALICE. *(interrupting)* Why was it called Hungarian if they sold Japanese?

JULIE. It was owned by Hungarians.

ALICE. *(quickly)* Got it. Go ahead ...

JULIE. ... so I'd tell him, "Mummy, can't you get your own..."

ALICE. *(interrupting again)* Hold it. I'm sorry. "Mummy"?

JULIE. His name was Mummy.

ALICE. This man. Your boss. Was named Mummy?

JULIE. Right.

ALICE. And he was Hungarian?

JULIE. French Morrocan.

ALICE. *(angrily)* Julie, are you making this up!!?

JULIE. *(exploding)* How could I make up something like this!!!? This is my life, Alice! This has been my life for the last ten years!

ALICE. My God, Julie. No wonder you're drinking.

JULIE. *(upset)* I'm unskilled. I'm untrained. I have no direction in my life. I'm totally unprepared for the real world.

ALICE. All right, so what kind of work are you interested in?

JULIE. I don't know.

ALICE. What'd you want to be when you were a little girl?

JULIE. I don't want to talk about it. It's embarrassing.

ALICE. You can tell me.

JULIE. It sounds awful.

ALICE. I won't tell anybody. Come on. Please? What'd you want to be as a girl?

JULIE. *(softly)* A wife. A mother.

ALICE. *(Beat. Takes a deep breath. Sadly.)* Me too. *(They sit a moment in silence. ALICE rises and goes over to her purse. She pulls out her little black book and hands it to JULIE.)*

JULIE. *(Opens it quickly and reads a name.)* Jackie Barnett. What's he like?

ALICE. He's a girl. *(JULIE rips out the page and crumples it. Throws it to the floor.)* Hey! She's a friend of mine. *(ALICE bends to retrieve the page.)*

JULIE. Bernie Cocoyannis.

ALICE. He's bald.

JULIE. So.

ALICE. He's a terrible kisser.

JULIE. We're not having him over here to neck. Shall I call him?

ALICE. Go ahead. He's probably home. He plays Bridge on Fridays with his mother. *(JULIE rips out the page and throws it to the floor.)* Hey, come on! *(ALICE bends to retrieve the crumpled page.)* Sometimes they need a fourth.

JULIE. What about this one?

ALICE. Which one?

JULIE. The one you crossed out here.

ALICE. He's a pervert. I met him on a bus.

JULIE. Why's he in here?

ALICE. He had a nice face. *(JULIE rips it out.)* He's perfect, Julie. He'd probably have a great time. We should call Jerry. He'd get a kick out of this too. *(ALICE reaches for the phone.)*

JULIE. *(stopping her)* Forget Jerry! That's why we're doing this. So you can forget about Jerry and get on with your life. I don't want some guy here to have a good time getting raped. We need a victim. Somebody who's vulnerable. *Attractive* but vulnerable. Somebody we can take advantage of.

ALICE. *(Points to a name.)* He's vulnerable. Cute too.

JULIE. Oh yeah?

ALICE. But he's only seven. *(ALICE laughs. JULIE doesn't.)* He's my nephew. Very cute kid. Wanna see a picture? *(JULIE stares at ALICE and very slowly rips the page out of the book. She hands it to ALICE.)*

ALICE. Thank you.

JULIE. *(Looks down at the phone book.)* What's this name?

ALICE. *(Looks at the book.)* Dustin Hoffman.

JULIE. What is Dustin Hoffman doing in your book?

ALICE. *(quickly)* Forget it. It means nothing. *(ripping the page out)* This girl claims she knows his dentist.

JULIE. What about this one?

ALICE. He's too Jewish.

JULIE. What's that mean?

ALICE. He reminds me of my grandmother. Always cooking for me. Does a great chicken. Let's call him.

JULIE. What about this one?

ALICE. He's gay.

JULIE. Why's he in here?

ALICE. *(defensively)* He's a friend. He's nice to talk to. *(JULIE rips out the last three pages of names and throws them to the floor.)* Hey, take it easy! You're eliminating my entire social life in one evening! *(ALICE bends down to pick up the crumpled pages.)* Oh God. I should've married young. I wouldn't have any of these problems. I'd probably be pregnant right now. Eating anything I wanted. Hot fudge sundaes. Lasagna. People would be begging me to eat. "It's for the child." "You need your strength." "Have another eclair." God, that would be wonderful! *(Beat. Looking up quickly.)* I didn't mean that! I don't want to be pregnant!

JULIE. Marshall Livingston III.

ALICE. My God, you're on the L's already?

JULIE. What's he like?

ALICE. How could you be on the L's? You must have skipped some. Let me see that. *(ALICE bends down and reads all the crumpled pages.)*

JULIE. Very classy. I like that name. Let's call him.

ALICE. *(Searches the black book frantically as JULIE dials.)* It took me three years to collect all these names and you've gone through half of them in four minutes! *(JULIE hands the phone to ALICE.)*

ALICE. *(Stares at JULIE. Impatiently.)* What!

JULIE. Say hello. Talk to him.

ALICE. *(angrily into phone)* Who is this? *(She turns to JULIE.)* He wants to know who I'm calling.

JULIE. Marshall Livingston III.

ALICE. *(into phone)* Is Marshall there? *(beat)* The third

one. *(beat)* Oh hi. I didn't recognize your voice. *(beat)* This is Alice *(beat)* Alice Meyerlink. *(beat)* Meyerlink. *(beat)* M.E.Y.E.R ... I met you in Alpha Beta about a month ago. In the Van De Kamps section. *(JULIE reacts. It's obvious ALICE hardly knows this guy.)* Yeah. Yeah, I'm short. That's the one. *(pause)* So. *(beat)* How've you been? *(beat)* That's good. *(beat)* Oh I've been fine. Yeah, I'm fine. I looked for you the last time I went to the store but I didn't see you. *(beat)* Yes, it is a big city, isn't it?

JULIE. Ask him to come over.

ALICE. Really? You did?

JULIE. Ask him to come over.

ALICE. *(giggles)* That's nice. That's really nice.

JULIE. Ask him to come over.

ALICE. *(to JULIE)* He thinks I'm cute.

JULIE. Would you ask him to come over!

ALICE. *(into phone)* Well as a matter of fact that's why I called. *(beat)* Umh huh. Umh huh. Umh huh. Umh huh...

JULIE. Is he coming over?

ALICE. *(to JULIE)* Shhh! *(into phone)* I'd love it! Yes! That's wonderful. Yes! *(Smiles at JULIE and gives her the OK sign.)* Let me give you the address. 6555 Lexington Avenue. Apartment 30. Right. OK. See you! *(Hangs up the phone and looks proudly at JULIE.)*

JULIE. Well?

ALICE. We have a lunch date on Tuesday.

JULIE. Jesus Christ!!!

(There's a loud knock at the door.)

JULIE. That was not the point of the phone call! *(JULIE moves to open the door.)*

(The PIZZA MAN is at the door.)

PIZZA MAN. Pizza Man. TONY

JULIE. *(to ALICE)* It's for you. *(ALICE bolts to the door and grabs the pizza. JULIE picks up the black book and searches through it. As ALICE begins to wolf down the pizza and JULIE searches for new names the PIZZA MAN stands ignored and awkwardly at the door.)*

PIZZA MAN. Umm ... *(He is in his late twenties and an average looking "fella." There is absolutely nothing outstanding about him. You could meet him on the street and forget you ever met him. But as he waits at the door for his money we sense a real vulnerability.)*

JULIE. *(reading from black book)* Ching Chang Ling. Who the hell is Ching Chang Ling?

ALICE. *(eating)* My dry cleaners.

PIZZA MAN. This is a nice apartment.

JULIE. Why would you put your dry cleaners in your little black book?

ALICE. I keep losing his card.

PIZZA MAN. What is it? A one bedroom?

JULIE. Arthur Orowitz.

ALICE. That's my grandfather.

JULIE. What's the purpose of a little black book if you put your dry cleaners and grandfather in it?

PIZZA MAN. Yep. This is real nice.

ALICE. I just wanted to fill the book. It doesn't look good empty.

JULIE. *(Throws the book on the couch and moves to pour herself another drink.)* Three years of socializing and you don't know one guy we can call.

ALICE. I'm sorry, Julie.

PIZZA MAN. You girls having a little party? (BEAT)

JULIE. *(There is an awkward pause. Suddenly she becomes aware of the young man at the door. She sets down the bottle of scotch. Looking over at him.)* Yes. *(moving closer)* Yes, we are.

PIZZA MAN. *(smiles)* Hey, all right.

JULIE. *(Stands very close to him and studies his face.)* What would they do to you if you didn't go back?

PIZZA MAN. Back?

JULIE. To your little pizza place.

PIZZA MAN. Hey, I got two pizzas in the truck. They'll get stiff.

JULIE. Stiff?

PIZZA MAN. Yeah, pizzas get real stiff real quickly.

JULIE. *(smiles)* I love it.

ALICE. *(Looks over at JULIE. Concerned.)* Julie.

JULIE. *(Stares at the young man for a moment. He stares back innocently and smiles. A beat. And JULIE moves away provocatively.)* Too bad! I was going to invite you in for a little drink. But! Duty calls. We don't want your little pizzas to get stiff. *(She pours herself a drink and toasts him.)*

PIZZA MAN. *(beat)* Well. If it's only one drink. *(beat)* I guess I could stay for one little drink.

JULIE. *(Smiles and crosses to him.)* That would be nice. *(She brings him into the apartment. He moves over to the couch and sits. She continues slowly.)* That would be very nice. *(ALICE*

with half a slice of pizza in her mouth stops eating and watches as
JULIE loudly bolt locks the front door.)

(The curtain closes ominously.)

END ACT ONE

ACT TWO
Scene One

The curtain opens to reveal the PIZZA MAN sitting very comfortably on the couch. His feet are stretched out on the coffee table. He is flanked by JULIE and ALICE who sit on the floor and look up at him as he finishes a long swallow of beer. There is a likeable cockiness about this young man as he is the center of attention now and appears to be enjoying it.

EDDIE. *(continuing what must be his life story)* ...So when I was in the Service I started thinking about what I wanted to do with my life. You think a lot of deep stuff like that when you're a man. And there's a war going on.

ALICE. *(transfixed)* My God. A war.

EDDIE. A lonely soldier in a strange land. Foreign people all around. Death lurking around every corner.

ALICE. Vietnam was awful.

EDDIE. Actually I was in Iceland.

ALICE. *(disappointed)* Oh.

EDDIE. *(quickly)* But the threat was still there! I *could've* been in 'Nam. Like that. *(snaps fingers)*.

ALICE. Really.

EDDIE. Oh yeah. I had a gun. We had guns.

ALICE. My God. Guns.

EDDIE. You get that close to Death you start to think about Life. I came back to the States and said to myself, "Eddie, boy. You got the whole pie in front of you. Go

46

out there and grab the biggest piece you can." You only go around once in Life. You gotta reach out with gusto.

ALICE. Absolutely. I've always said that.

EDDIE. So I bought a van and started delivering pizzas.

ALICE. And you've been delivering pizzas ever since.

EDDIE. Oh no. Hell no. I tried a lot of things. One year I was a promotional manager for beef jerky. But I didn't like the pressure. Did you ever notice how many brands of beef jerky there are?

ALICE. Yes.

EDDIE. It's a cut-throat business. Life's too short for that kind of pressure. You gotta enjoy Life while you can. While you still got a couple of arms and legs. So I grew a beard and went back to pizzas.

ALICE. *(amazed)* You grew a beard?

EDDIE. *(proudly)* Oh yeah.

ALICE. I can't imagine you with a beard.

EDDIE. *(smiling)* You know Kris Kristofferson?

ALICE. *(impressed)* You looked like Kris Kristofferson?

EDDIE. Better.

ALICE. Wow.

EDDIE. I was gonna keep it but the third month I got a rash.

ALICE. *(sadly)* A rash.

EDDIE. I put calomine lotion on it but it kept clotting. It made me look like a sloppy eater so I cut it.

ALICE. A blessing! You have such a wholesome face you shouldn't hide it under a lot of hair. *(to JULIE)*

Doesn't he have a wholesome face? *(JULIE stares at EDDIE. She hasn't taken her eyes off of him during the entire inane conversation.)* A good, clean, wholesome, *nice* face.

JULIE. He's perfect.

EDDIE. Thanks.

ALICE. Julie, no!

JULIE. He's so perfect.

EDDIE. *(beaming)* Thanks a lot.

ALICE. *(whispering to JULIE)* We can't do this!

EDDIE. *(naively)* Do what?

JULIE. But he's so perfect.

ALICE. Julie, he's a nice guy. He's a veteran.

JULIE. So.

ALICE. I can't do something that awful to a veteran.

EDDIE. *(getting nervous)* Do what?

JULIE. Alice, it's fate.

ALICE. Fate?

JULIE. We have to do it. If we weren't supposed to do it we wouldn't have found someone to do it to. But he's perfect for it so we've got to do it.

EDDIE. *(frantically)* Do what? Perfect to do what?!!!

JULIE. *(Moves up to the couch quickly. She sits very close to EDDIE. Seriously.)* Do you believe in God?

EDDIE. Huh?

JULIE. Do you believe in things like that?

EDDIE. *(confused)* I think so. Yeah. Why?

JULIE. We were just discussing how sometimes if you're not sure you should do something you get a sign making it easy for you to do it.

EDDIE. *(Stares at JULIE.)* Do what?

JULIE. *(She just stares at EDDIE. Not sure how to begin this rape. She looks down at the floor, at ALICE, for assistance.)* Alice, give me a little help here.

ALICE. What? *(JULIE motions ALICE to sit on the other side of EDDIE. After a confused beat she moves up to the couch. To EDDIE.)* Hi *(The young man turns to ALICE and watches her curiously.)* I'm glad you believe in God.

EDDIE. *(Looks at ALICE; then JULIE.)* Are you girls a religious sect?

ALICE. Oh no. Julie never goes to church. And I'm Jewish. Are you a practologist?

EDDIE. What?

ALICE. Do you practice some denomination?

EDDIE. I used to. I was in Catholic School as a kid. I even went into the seminary to be a priest.

ALICE. Oh Julie, he's a priest! *(She starts to move away from him quickly.)*

EDDIE. No, I'm not. I dropped out.

ALICE. *(moving closer)* Oh I'm sorry. What happened?

EDDIE. There's more to Life than religion. Life's too short to spend it behind a collar. You gotta reach out with gusto. *(quietly)* And my girlfriend got pregnant.

ALICE. Oh.

EDDIE. Yeah.

ALICE. So you left to find out who did it.

EDDIE. I did it.

ALICE. You did it?

EDDIE. Yeah.

ALICE. *(amazed)* I didn't know you could do that in the seminary.

EDDIE. We didn't do it in the seminary. We did it in my car.

ALICE. *(really amazed)* I didn't know you could have cars in the seminary.

EDDIE. Oh yeah. Sure.

ALICE. Did you know that, Julie? Did you know they have cars in the seminary? *(Deciding there's too much conversation and not enough "action" JULIE makes her first move. She places her hand on the young man's thigh. EDDIE looks at it. So does ALICE.)*

ALICE. *(A beat. Decides to move on.)* Anyway. *(She looks away.)* So you quit being a priest after your girlfriend got pregnant.

EDDIE. No, I wasn't a priest yet. *(JULIE rubs his leg slowly.)*

ALICE. *(Chooses to ignore now whatever happens at the other end of the couch. She thinks if she keeps talking everything will be fine. Nervously.)* What were you then? What *was* it that you were called? A pre-priest? Were you a pre-priest?

EDDIE. I was a... *(JULIE nuzzles his ear.)* ...I was just ... uh ... *(JULIE moves in closer.)* ...you know... *(JULIE nibbles his ear.)* ...We had... *(grabbing his ear)* DAMNITT!! *(to JULIE)* You bit my ear! *(to ALICE)* She bit my ear!

ALICE. Julie, that was very rude.

EDDIE. *(to JULIE)* What's the matter with you? *(JULIE starts to unbutton his shirt.)*

ALICE. *(Looks quickly the other way. Moving right along.)* So. You got kicked out of the seminary and then what happened?

EDDIE. *(watching JULIE)* I got drafted.

ALICE. And the girl you knocked up?

EDDIE. We got married. *(to JULIE)* What are you doing?

JULIE. *(softly)* Unbuttoning your shirt.

ALICE. *(Her eyes widen.)* Married?

EDDIE. *(to JULIE)* Why?

JULIE. *(coyly)* You look warm.

ALICE. You got married?

JULIE. Don't you feel warm?

ALICE. *(as a lawyer)* How long ago was this you were married?

EDDIE. *(to ALICE)* 10 years. *(to JULIE)* I feel fine.

JULIE. Nonsense. You're perspiring. Are you nervous?

ALICE. Is this girl still around? The one you married?

EDDIE. *(answering ALICE)* Yes.

JULIE. *(thinking he answered her)* Why are you nervous?

EDDIE. *(nervous)* I'm not nervous.

ALICE. So I guess then you're still married then.

JULIE. Your lips are quivering.

EDDIE. *(tight-lipped)* My lips *never* quiver.

ALICE. *Are* you still married?

EDDIE. *(trying to control his lips)* Never.

ALICE. *(confused)* What?

JULIE. Shall I kiss them and make them stop?

EDDIE. No.

ALICE. You're *not* married?

EDDIE. *(to ALICE)* Yes. *(JULIE moves in closer.)*

ALICE. Yes, you *are* married? *(JULIE starts to kiss him.)*

EDDIE. No!

ALICE. You're *not* married? *(JULIE kisses him. A long*

kiss.) Are you married? *(The kiss continues.)* Hello. *(He mumbles something.)* What? I can't hear you. Julie, this is important. *(She pulls them apart.)* Are you married?

EDDIE. Yes!

ALICE. *(Stares at him. Indignant.)* You're a married man and you're kissing another woman! *(to JULIE)* He's perfect! *(ALICE kisses him hard.)*

EDDIE. *(He breaks away.)* What the hell?!

ALICE. Go ahead and give me the line about Yucatan and the Natives!!! *(ALICE pounces on him and pins him down on the couch.)* Tell me how much you love me and then DUMP me!!!

EDDIE. Hey, look. I gotta get back to the truck. My pizzas are getting stiff.

ALICE. *(holding him down)* That's *your* problem! I'm running this. I, Alice Meyerlink, am finally on top! How do you like it down there, huh? *(He's having trouble breathing.)* Do you know I was never claustrophobic until I started having sex!!!

JULIE. *(Quickly hands ALICE a handkerchief. Businesslike.)* Stick this in his mouth in case he screams.

EDDIE. *(panicked)* Screams?!!! *(He bolts from the couch. JULIE moves slowly, ominously towards him. ALICE also begins to stalk him and he backs away from them cautiously.)* Hey, you guys. I gotta get back to work. *(The girls stalk him around the couch.)*

JULIE. You can't leave now. We're just getting to know each other.

EDDIE. I'll lose my job.

JULIE. Did anybody ever tell you you've got a great ass.

EDDIE. *(laughs nervously)* Hey, that's cute! I really like you guys, you know? *(starts for door)* But I gotta leave.

JULIE. *(She blocks him.)* What're you trying to pull here anyway? You knew what you were getting into when you walked in here.

EDDIE. No, I didn't! Honest to *God!* I didn't!

JULIE. No decent man would've walked into a strange woman's apartment flaunting his body the way you do.

EDDIE. Flaunting?

JULIE. Look at your tight pants. You're just asking for trouble, Mister.

EDDIE. Hey, give me a break!

ALICE. You don't even wear a wedding band, you schmuck!!! *(She lunges at him.)*

EDDIE. *(He bolts for the door and tries to open it. But it's locked. ALICE attacks him as he fumbles with the lock.)* Let me out of here, DAMNITT!!!

ALICE. *(Struggles with him.)* That's right WALK OUT! Go back to your wife! You're all alike, you know that? *(He pushes her away and she stumbles back against the couch.)* When things start getting tough you turn *CHICKEN* and walk out!!!

EDDIE. *(He hesitates at the door. Beat. He turns slowly and stares at ALICE. Quietly.)* What did you say?

ALICE. Men are all alike. As soon as the relationship starts getting tough and they can't run it they walk out. You're all CHICKEN! *(EDDIE moves over to ALICE slowly. Threateningly. It scares her. She continues meekly.)* Julie?

EDDIE. *(quietly angry)* Nobody calls me chicken. I *almost* saw combat. *(He turns to JULIE. Suddenly he's in charge.)* Can

I use your phone? *(JULIE nods timidly. EDDIE moves over to the phone and dials quickly. The women exchange puzzled looks. On the phone. Very businesslike.)* Hank. This is Eddie. I got a little action on the Special. Double cheese, double anchovies. Hold the onions. *(beat)* Yeah, well there's two of them so I don't know how long it'll take. *(He smiles.)* Yeah, well. *(beat)* OK. I'll come in early Saturday. Thanks, Hank. I owe you one. *(He hangs up.)* OK, it's all set.

JULIE. What is?

EDDIE. All I gotta do is dump off these last two pizzas and I'll be right back.

JULIE. Back?

EDDIE. You girls abviously want a little action so I cleared it with the boss.

ALICE. You cleared it with the boss?

EDDIE. It happens all the time. It's what you call an occupational hazard. Some guys have to wear hard hats. *(He smiles.)* We have to wear hard ...

ALICE. *(interrupting)* You cleared it with your boss?!!!

EDDIE. We always got extra guys to cover at night so it's cool. I'll just drop these two pizzas and I'll be right back. Can I use your john? Beer goes right through me. *(The two women just stare at him in shock.)*

EDDIE. *(He waits a moment for them to answer but they continue to stare.)* I'll find it. *(He exits into the bedroom.)*

ALICE. *(Silence. Quietly.)* He cleared it with his boss? *(beat)* He has such a nice, wholesome face.

JULIE. It's off!

ALICE. What is?

JULIE. The rape. It's all off.

ALICE. Why?

JULIE. He's the wrong type.

ALICE. Julie, he's perfect. He's a married man and he's gonna have a menage-a-twat. He's twice as bad as Jerry.

JULIE. But he's gonna enjoy it! He'll probably have a great time and then go back and tell his boss. We'll have every pizza man in the city here.

ALICE. *(Thinks a moment.)* Could we get free pizzas that way?

JULIE. It's all off. *(pouring a drink)* The whole purpose of a rape is to catch somebody offguard. You can't be trying to rape somebody and they say to you, "Just a minute. I have to drop off some pizzas." It doesn't work that way!

ALICE. Well, we're new at this.

JULIE. Hold it.

ALICE. What?

JULIE. That's it!

ALICE. What?

JULIE. Have we got any rope?

ALICE. Rope? Why do we need rope? *(JULIE frantically begins to search the living room. ALICE continues nervously.)* Julie. Why is it we need rope?

JULIE. We don't need rope.

ALICE. *(relieved)* No, we don't. Definitely we don't. Rope sounds dangerous. We definitely don't need rope.

JULIE. We can use an extension cord. *(as she searches for one)*

ALICE. *(panicked)* Julie, is this dangerous?

JULIE. *(Finds an extension cord.)* OK, now look...

ALICE. I won't do this if it's dangerous.

JULIE. When he comes out of the bathroom you hit him low and I'll hit him high.

ALICE. *This* is dangerous.

JULIE. We'll catch him offguard. He thinks he's gonna walk right out of here and deliver those pizzas. But we're not gonna let him.

ALICE. We're not?

JULIE. We're gonna tie him up and put him on the couch. Then we're in charge again. And he can't do a thing about it.

ALICE. We're gonna tie him up on the couch?

JULIE. Yes.

ALICE. With the extension cord we use for the Christmas tree?

JULIE. Right.

ALICE. I think I'll pass on this. *(Heads for the bedroom.)*

JULIE. Alice!

ALICE. No, really. This is getting too physical. And I'm very tired. *(yawns quickly)* And I should go to bed. Goodnight. *(heading towards the bedroom)*

JULIE. Alice. He's a married man. *(ALICE suddenly stops. JULIE continues dramatically.)* We're probably not his first.

ALICE. *(Turns back.)* *I'll* hit him high. *You* hit him low. *(She takes the extension cord from JULIE.)*

(We hear the bathroom door open and close.)

JULIE. Kill the lights. *(They kill the lights.)*

ALICE. *(Beat. Quietly.)* Julie.

JULIE. *(whispering)* What?

ALICE. I have to go to the bathroom.

JULIE. Shhh!

ALICE. Really bad.

JULIE. Alice, for god's sake!

ALICE. I can't help it. Something happens to my bladder when it gets dark. I could never play Hide and Seek as a kid.

(We hear the hall door opening.)

JULIE. Shhh! he's coming.

ALICE. Tell him to hurry.

(EDDIE comes into the darkened living room.)

EDDIE. Hey! What happened to the lights? *(beat)* Come on, you guys. I can't see. *(beat)* I told you I gotta deliver those pizzas. It'll take ten minutes. We got all night to do stuff like this. But business before pleasure. You know what I mean? Let's just turn on the old lights here and...

JULIE. NOW!!!

EDDIE. What the hell?!!!

(We hear the sounds of bodies falling to the floor and loud struggling.)

EDDIE. OW!!! GODDAMNITT!!!

ALICE. My God! My God!

JULIE. Shit!

(There is more struggling. A lamp falls over. A chair. The noise seems to be moving across stage to the couch. Suddenly a light clicks on. We see ALICE lying on the couch with the extension cord partially wrapped around her and JULIE pinning her down. The PIZZA MAN lies dazed on the floor beneath them.)

JULIE. *(to ALICE)* What're you doing?!!!

ALICE. I hit low.

JULIE. You were supposed to hit high!

ALICE. I thought you said low.

EDDIE. *(starting to get up)* You guys are crazy. I'm getting out of here.

ALICE. *(to JULIE)* I distinctly remember you telling me... *(JULIE leaps at EDDIE; grabbing an object from the end table. She smashes it hard against his head. He falls to the floor and doesn't move. The two women stare at his motionless body. ALICE continues quietly.)* Oh my God. *(beat)* You killed him.

JULIE. *(Turns pale.)* I didn't want him to leave. He was gonna leave.

ALICE. You didn't have to kill him.

JULIE. *(Bends over him.)* He's not dead. I just knocked him out.

ALICE. *(relieved)* Oh good. He's just knocked out. Just knocked out. *(There is an awkward beat as the two girls stare down at the unconscious PIZZA MAN. ALICE turns slowly to JULIE.)* Now what? *(beat)* Now what do we do?

JULIE. *(quietly)* I don't know. *(slowly)* But we'll think of something. *(They struggle with EDDIE. Lifting him and putting him on the couch.)*

(Music in. Fade to black.)

END ACT TWO SCENE ONE

Scene Two

The lights come up to reveal the now-conscious EDDIE bound and gagged on the couch. His hands are tied behind him. His feet are tied with the extension cord. JULIE sits downstage in semi-darkness chain smoking. ALICE is center stage wearing a makeshift and "suggestive" outfit. She boredly keeps time with the music, swaying her hips in an attempt to vamp the PIZZA MAN. But it's clear her heart isn't into it. After a few moments the music fades.

ALICE. *(to JULIE)* Do I have to keep wearing this?

JULIE. Yes.

ALICE. I feel so cheap. *(flops on couch)* I don't even know this guy. *(to EDDIE)* I don't even know you. What was your name again? *(He mumbles something unintelligible.)* This is boring. I'm doing all the work and he's just sitting there. *(noticing JULIE just sitting)* And *you're* just sitting there. I'm doing the bumping and the grinding and the two of you are just sitting there!

JULIE. Put on that Barry White album again. I thought I heard him groan once.

ALICE. Julie, this is hopeless. I've tried everything. Dancing. Nibbling. Carressing. He's already fallen asleep once! *(EDDIE mumbles again.)* Can't we ungag him?

JULIE. No!

ALICE. Why not?

JULIE. You take the tape off and he's gonna start screaming.

ALICE. He won't scream. Why would he scream? *(to EDDIE)* You wouldn't scream, would you? *(EDDIE mumbles something.)*

JULIE. *(her frustration mounting)* SHUT UP!!! *(EDDIE immediately stops mumbling.)*

ALICE. *(Silence. Quietly.)* Julie, this isn't working.

JULIE. *(angrily)* I know that!

ALICE. Maybe if he could talk to us he can tell us what his problem is. *(confidentially)* Maybe he has a war wound.)

JULIE. *(Stares at EDDIE for a moment. She crosses over to him. Che Guevara in command...)* All right, look. If we take this off, are you gonna scream? *(EDDIE shakes his head.)* You promise? I'm trusting you now. You promise not to scream? *(EDDIE nods. To ALICE.)* OK. Take it off. *(ALICE rips off the tape quickly. EDDIE screams in agony. JULIE pounces on him and covers his mouth with her hand. To ALICE.)* You see!

ALICE. *(quickly)* Julie, that was a pain scream, not a help scream.

JULIE. It was a scream! We can't have screaming! Give me the tape.

ALICE. No.

JULIE. Give me the tape!

ALICE. NO!

JULIE. Are you gonna give me that tape?!

ALICE. *(reminding her)* No screaming.

JULIE. Give me the goddamn tape!!!

ALICE. Julie, this isn't like us to let a man come between our friendship.

JULIE. You want me to sit here all night with my hand in his mouth?

ALICE. Let me talk to him, all right?

JULIE. I'm not moving.

ALICE. *(Moves in close to EDDIE. Urgently...)* Look, Eddie. It is Eddie? Isn't it Eddie? *(He nods. ALICE puts an arm around his shoulder. Bargaining with him.)* I like you, Eddie. I think basically you're a nice person. I *am* a little disappointed that you're cheating on your wife... *(EDDIE mumbles something. ALICE corrects herself.)* ...Thinking about cheating on your wife. But I'll overlook that right now because I have to have your solemn word you will not scream. There's a lot of old people in this building and they're very bothered by anonymous screaming. So you must promise me there will be no screaming. *(confidentially)* And I'll get you out of this as soon as I can.

JULIE. *(quickly)* No bargaining.

ALICE. I'll *try* to get you out of here as soon as I can. All right, Eddie? *(He nods.)*

JULIE. *(Hesitates for a beat. She glares at ALICE. Slowly.)* If he screams... *(She slowly removes her hand from his mouth.)*

EDDIE. *(Beat. Whispering.)* Could I have a glass of water?

ALICE. Sure. *(Starts towards the kitchen.)*

JULIE. No! No water.

ALICE. Julie, he's thirsty.

JULIE. No water until he cooperates.

ALICE. That's not fair. I'm sure he's doing the best he can.

EDDIE. Look, I'm sorry.

JULIE. What's the matter with you anyway? This poor girl has been working on you for over an hour. Now, what's the problem?!

EDDIE. I don't know. This has never happened before.

ALICE. *(respectfully)* Is it a war wound?

EDDIE. *(angrily)* I was in Iceland!

ALICE. *(quickly)* I'm sorry. It slipped my mind.

EDDIE. I guess I'm a little nervous.

ALICE. How about a nice cup of tea? Tea's very relaxing.

EDDIE. I can't understand it. *(desperate)* Look, don't tell anybody about this, all right? I've never had this problem before. Never! I'm fine. I always do fine!

ALICE. That's all right, Eddie. *(She puts his head on her shoulder.)* It's OK. Go ahead and cry.

EDDIE. *(quickly)* I'm not crying.

ALICE. It's nothing to be ashamed of. It's very beautiful when a man cries.

EDDIE. I'm not crying.

ALICE. Why are your eyes wet?

EDDIE. *(angrily)* You mauled me when you ripped off the tape!

ALICE. *(to JULIE)* It *was* a pain scream.

EDDIE. *(angrily)* It's a reflex, that's all! A pain reflex. You pluck a hair from your nose and your eyes water.

ALICE. I *never* pluck my nose.

EDDIE. *(adamant)* But it's *not* crying. I'm not crying. I *don't* cry.

ALICE. You don't?

EDDIE. *No.*

ALICE. Never. Not even at funerals?

EDDIE. *Never.*

ALICE. Well, *that's* your problem.

EDDIE. *(defensively)* What problem? I don't have a problem!

ALICE. Your little sexual problem. Julie hasn't cried in years and look at the mess she's in.

JULIE. *(defensively)* What mess? I'm not in any mess!

ALICE. I don't understand how you people can go through Life without crying. I can't make it through a day sometimes. It's not healthy. It causes diseases. *(to EDDIE)* When's the last time you cried?

EDDIE. What?

ALICE. *(with great urgency)* Approximately. Give or take a few weeks.

EDDIE. I don't know. It's not important.

ALICE. *(impatiently)* Please, Eddie I'm trying to help you.

EDDIE. I don't remember. Nine or ten.

ALICE. Nine or ten what? Years. Months?

EDDIE. I was a kid. I was nine or ten.

ALICE. *(Stares at him.)* You haven't cried since you were nine?

EDDIE. Or ten.

ALICE. *(concerned)* Oh Eddie. You're not well, are you?

EDDIE. *(angrily)* I feel fine!

JULIE. What made you cry?

EDDIE. *(Looks at JULIE. He is reluctant to tell them.)* I don't know. It was a long time ago.

JULIE. *(impatiently)* Come on. What was it?

EDDIE. *(Takes a beat. With great difficulty...)* I was a ... pitcher ... for our Pee-Wee League Team ... And we lost. *(The women look at EDDIE and wait for him to continue.)*

ALICE. Yes? *(beat)* And then what happened? What made you cry?

EDDIE. *(incredulously)* We lost the game! *(The women continue to stare at EDDIE. Unable to comprehend why something so insignificant could bring on tears.)* You guys never played ball? *(They shake their heads.)* What about P.E.?

ALICE. I always took folk dancing.

EDDIE. *(Stares at them in disbelief.)* The thrill of success. The agony of defeat. You don't know about all that?

JULIE. No.

EDDIE. *(speechless)* Gee. *(He stares at the two women. Unable to comprehend the tremendous distance between them. Patiently he attempts to explain..)* It was our championship game. I was under a lot of pressure. I was only nine.

ALICE. Or ten.

EDDIE. We were ahead by three. In the sixth inning they got ten runs off me. We never caught up. I felt it was my fault we lost the game. I let the team down. So afterwards I started crying. I wasn't bawling or anything like that ... But the tears were kinda rolling down my face. I hid behind the bleachers so nobody'd see me. But my dad came back there and caught me. He got really mad and threw a mitt in my face. Really hard. He said I was a baby. Men don't cry.

ALICE. And you stopped crying?

EDDIE. No! He broke my nose. It hurt like hell! *(beat)-* But I never cried after that.

JULIE. What do you do now when you feel like crying?

EDDIE. I clear my throat. *(He clears his throat.)*

ALICE. *(quickly)* You wanna cry?

EDDIE. No!

ALICE. You cleared your throat.

EDDIE. I was just showing you!

ALICE. Maybe if you had a good cry you could solve your sexual problem and we...

EDDIE. *(angrily)* I DON'T HAVE A SEXUAL PROBLEM! *(He struggles.)* Untie me, goddamnitt I'll show you! I'll show you how good I am!

JULIE. We don't want you to do good. That's not what we're doing here.

EDDIE. What *are* we doing here? I don't know what the hell's going on. You girls wanted action; I said sure. Next thing I know I'm tied up and made to feel guilty cause I can't perform.

JULIE. Do you know the statistics for rape?

EDDIE. *(beat)* Rape?

JULIE. A rape is committed every seven minutes. We've been working on you for over an hour. Now, something's got to be wrong. Newsweek never lies.

EDDIE. What do you mean rape? What do you mean by that?

ALICE. We're raping you. We're *trying* to rape you.

EDDIE. *(Stares at the two women.)* Is this a sorority prank?

JULIE. *(serious)* We're dead serious. *(He looks at ALICE.)*

ALICE. *(shrugs)* It was her idea. *(EDDIE begins to laugh loudly.)*

JULIE. What's so funny?

EDDIE. You can't rape me.

JULIE. Why not?

EDDIE. I'm a man.

JULIE. So what.

EDDIE. A woman can't rape a man. It's physically impossible. The only way you can rape me is if I'm willing to cooperate. And if I cooperate it isn't a rape. So you might as well untie me and forget the whole stupid idea.

ALICE. *(rising)* Well, goodnight.

JULIE. Sit down, Alice.

ALICE. Julie, he's right. There's nothing we can do about it. We've been cheated by Nature.

JULIE. Sit down! *(ALICE dejectedly sits next to EDDIE.)*

JULIE. *(Moves over to the couch and sits on the other side of EDDIE. Quietly.)* You think you're pretty smart, don't you? You're real cocky.

EDDIE. *(smiles)* Well. When you're right you're right.

JULIE. *(smiling)* You think so, huh?

EDDIE. I know so.

JULIE. Sooner or later you're gonna get a sexy thought. It's inevitable. You can't fight it. It's part of having a "Y" chromosome. And when that sexy thought hits you we're gonna jump on you.

EDDIE. That's stupid. Sometimes I don't get a sexy thought for two ... three hours.

JULIE. We'll wait.

ALICE. We will?

JULIE. If we have to sit up all night we'll wait.

ALICE. All night? *(beat)* Should I make coffee?

EDDIE. I'd like a cup.

JULIE. No coffee!!! Nothing! We're just gonna sit here and wait. *(She folds her arms and looks down in the direction of EDDIE's jeans.)*

ALICE. *(There is an awkward silence.)* Does anybody want to watch the "Tonight Show"? *(silence)* No, I don't really want to watch it either. Actually I think people watch entirely too much television. Very few people could do what we're doing right now. Just sitting here like this. Talking. *(silence)* I hate silence. Could we put on some music?

JULIE. Alice. Just sit there and stop talking. *(Beat. ALICE sits back dejectedly like a disciplined child.)*

EDDIE. How come you guys are doing something like this? I mean you seem like such nice girls.

ALICE. *(smiles)* Thank you.

JULIE. Flattery won't help.

EDDIE. Are you guys some kind of feminists?

ALICE. *(angrily)* Of course not! We're strictly heterosexual.

EDDIE. I don't think you have to be gay to be one of those.

ALICE. I've seen them on Phil Donohue. They all look like truck drivers and they never smile.

EDDIE. I think some of the things they say are pretty good.

JULIE. Whose asking you?

EDDIE. If a woman does the same work as a man I think she should get the same pay. I'm all for that.

JULIE. That's big of you.

EDDIE. Of course there are certain things that a woman can't do like a man can.

JULIE. *(quickly)* Like what? Go ahead and name one!

EDDIE. *(Thinks a moment.)* Rape.

JULIE. If you say one more word I'll put the tape back on.

ALICE. He does have a point, Julie.

JULIE. Alice. Don't help.

ALICE. *(to EDDIE)* Have you ever tried to rape a girl?

EDDIE. Are you kidding? Rape's for people who can't get any on their own. When's the last time you guys got laid?

JULIE. Hand me that tape! Give me the tape!!

ALICE. Julie, no!

JULIE. I'm not gonna sit here and be insulted by a Pizza Man.

EDDIE. Hey, I'm sorry. I didn't mean to insult you.

ALICE. That's all right, Eddie, It's a valid question.

EDDIE. I'm only trying to help.

ALICE. I know. I know.

EDDIE. I mean if you're horny you're horny. A good fuck could help.

JULIE. *(angrily)* Alice, I'm gonna hit him!!!

EDDIE. Relax! What's the matter with you?

ALICE. Look, Eddie. Could we just call it "nookie, nookie"? It has a nice sound and it never offends anyone.

EDDIE. Call it what you like. I don't care.

ALICE. It's just that men use different words for it than women and it's offensive to us. I mean it's very difficult for a woman to discuss it with a man anyway. Especially a strange man like yourself. Can you understand that?

EDDIE. Sure.

ALICE. Good. *(beat)* The last time I was nooked was a week ago Tuesday. Julie?

JULIE. What?

ALICE. The man asked you a question.

JULIE. I'm not going to tell him the last time I had sex.

ALICE. She's very shy about these things.

JULIE. It's none of his business.

ALICE. *(confidentially)* Julie doesn't date much.

EDDIE. *(knowingly)* Oh!

JULIE. What does that mean?

EDDIE. Well, you know. I read about those things.

JULIE. What things?

EDDIE. I know how difficult it gets for a woman when she gets older. *(JULIE stares at him.)* A guy gets older and he can always pay for it. But it must be very tough when you're a woman. I can see why you don't wanna talk about it.

JULIE. *(interrupting)* The last time I had sex was this afternoon. It was approximately 3:00 and it was a brief but titillating experience with the Edison Man.

ALICE. I don't think I know him. Does he live in the building?

JULIE. He reads our meter.

ALICE. Oh. I thought his name was "Edison." He works for the Edison *Company.*

JULIE. Yes.

ALICE. I didn't know you were dating him.

JULIE. I'm not. He came to read the meter and we just did it.

ALICE. *(Stares at JULIE.)* You made nookie nookie with the meter reader.

JULIE. Yes.

ALICE. *(shocked)* My God, Julie! That's awful! That's not like you. That's awful! You've *never* done anything like that before. Never! *(beat)* Have you?

JULIE. Never.

ALICE. Never! Never have you done something like that! It's filthy!

EDDIE. And cheap.

JULIE. Stay out of this.

ALICE. Filthy and cheap. *Cheap* and filthy. It's disgusting. *(beat)* How was it?

JULIE. Short.

ALICE. No, how was the nookie nookie?

JULIE. It was short. Brief. He spent more time with the meter than me.

ALICE. *(Stares at JULIE with sad disgust.)* Julie, why? Why would you do something like that?

JULIE. *(Moves away and pours herself a drink.)* I'm tired of Single's bars. Of going to parties with people I don't know who are there for the same reason I am. I'm bored with Friday night movies and bad Chinese restaurants. And chit chat and having to be pleasant. I just wanted to *do it* and get it over with. It was an impulse. *(beat)* A humiliating impulse.

EDDIE. Yeah. Easy lays are the worst.

JULIE. It wasn't easy, believe me.

EDDIE. Not for you. You're still brooding about it. But he's probably at some bar right now bragging.

ALICE. Oh God, Julie. We're gonna have Edison men

here every day. Edison men and Pizza men. Things like this spread. We'll have every public servant in the city here!

EDDIE. That's a good point. Maybe you better untie me and forget about all this.

JULIE. No! You're different. I don't want you to enjoy it. I want you to feel what it's like to be taken advantage of. I want you to see how it is to be used and then *dumped.*

EDDIE. *(to ALICE)* Is she always this uptight?

ALICE. Sometimes during her period. Is it your period, Julie?

JULIE. No.

ALICE. *(confidentially)* She's had a bad day. She lost her job. *(JULIE turns quickly and stares at ALICE.)*

EDDIE. Oh hey. Bummer.

JULIE. *(to ALICE)* You've got a big mouth, you know that?

ALICE. Well, you told him you had sex with the Edison Man!

EDDIE. I'm sorry about your job.

JULIE. You're not sorry. You don't even know me.

EDDIE. I know how it is. Unemployment is a bummer. You gotta stand in line and they always say your name wrong. Look, if you want I can talk to my boss. He's always looking for girls to take orders over the phone.

JULIE. *(Stares at him incredulously.)* I'm 28 years old. I was almost a college graduate!

EDDIE. We can train anybody.

JULIE. I was voted "Most Likely to Succeed" in high school. And you want me to take a job pushing pizzas?!

EDDIE. Come on. Everybody's hot stuff in high school.

JULIE. Oh yeah?

EDDIE. Yeah.

JULIE. *(quickly)* What was your grade point average?

EDDIE. I don't remember.

JULIE. Mine was 3.85. All four years.

EDDIE. I got straight A's in Shop.

JULIE. I got straight A's my whole Junior year.

EDDIE. *(quickly)* Did you ever run for office?

JULIE. *Many* times.

EDDIE. You're looking at the President of the Holy Cross Club.

JULIE. Treasurer of my Sophomore Class. Secretary of my Junior Class. Vice President of my Senior Class. And first woman President of the entire school!

ALICE. I was in the band.

EDDIE. But did you play football?

JULIE. I was a cheerleader.

EDDIE. *I* played football!

JULIE. I dated the football team! And the basketball team. Several swimmers. And a broad jumper!

ALICE. I played the clarinet.

EDDIE. So big deal. You were a big deal in high school. *(beat)* Sometimes things don't work out as good as you think they will. But that's life. You take it on the chin and move on. *(quietly)* I've accepted the fact I'm never gonna be a Bishop.

ALICE. Oh Eddie. You wanted to be a Bishop?

EDDIE. That's all right. I've adjusted. I've still got some dreams. I'm learning a lot about the food business.

Maybe someday I'll open my own place. A small cafe.
Homecooking and fresh pies. *(proudly)* Maybe a little
truck stop.

JULIE. A truck stop? Your dream now is a truck
stop?

EDDIE. A guy's gotta have dreams. You gotta believe
in something.

JULIE. And you believe in a truck stop?

EDDIE. It's something.

ALICE. If people didn't believe in fairies Tinker Bell
would've died.

EDDIE. That's true.

ALICE. Pinocchio would still be a wooden doll.
Dumbo would never have flown.

EDDIE. That's right.

ALICE. You've got to believe in something, Julie.

JULIE. I've spent 28 years believing. I followed the
rules. Did everything I was supposed to do. I'm a good
person. I'm a nice girl. And where am I? *NOWHERE.*
And what have I got? NOTHING!

ALICE. An attitude like that would've killed Tinker
Bell.

JULIE. *(exploding)* I'm not talking about fairy tales! I'm
talking about REAL LIFE! ... You wanna know what life
is? It's pain and suffering. It's getting kicked in the teeth
and having to get up and keep going ... But nobody told
us that when we were kids. They gave us fairy tales.
Handed us dreams and shoved us into the streets and
said keep smiling. Everything'll be fine! Well, kiddos
we're not kiddos anymore. And the dreams don't work!
Forget about your truck stops, Yucatans, true love,

marriages that work, happiness ever after, and look at what we are! *(Turns to EDDIE quickly.)* You knocked up a girl. Flunked out of a seminary ... You wanted to be a Bishop, for crissakes. And now you're a delivery boy. A Pizza Man pushing 30!

EDDIE. *(softly)* I'm only 29.

JULIE. *(turning to ALICE quickly)* You're fat. Neurotic. You work at a crummy insurance company you claim isn't that bad. But you'll believe *anything* any man tells you because maybe he might marry you and carry you away from that insurance job you claim isn't that bad!

ALICE. *(quietly)* Well, nobody's perfect.

JULIE. And I drink. *(Pours herself another scotch.)* Because I understand all of this. And with all my insight. All this knowledge. I'm still a failure.

ALICE. You're not a failure.

JULIE. Yes, I am. A rape is commited every seven minutes. He's been here for three hours and he's still wearing his pants.

ALICE. Oh my God. We forgot to take off your pants.

JULIE. I'm unemployed. I've had ten jobs in the last eight years. I live in a crappy one-bedroom apartment I can't afford to furnish. And I don't even have a husband I can blame it on. *(She drinks.)* I was the girl who had everything. Looks, intelligence. A smile. God, what a smile! It used to get me anything I wanted. Cheerleader. The best looking boys ... *(with great respect)* "THE OPTIMIST CLUB AWARD." We had to write an essay for that. And I wrote, "Anything in life can be accomplished with a smile!" They gave me a plaque and voted me "Most Likely to Succeed." It worked for me in high school, it would work for me in life. I used to walk down the street smiling at everybody. Most people never looked at me. The rest tried to pick me up. Perverts. Lesbians. And cops who thought I was a hooker because perverts and lesbians were trying to pick me up. *(She drinks.)* So one day I stopped smiling. I don't remember where. I don't remember when. I just reached for my smile and it wasn't there. *(turning to EDDIE)* But if you look close you can see the wrinkles from when I used to smile. From all the years of smiling when I didn't feel like it. At jokes that weren't funny. And people I didn't like. Men who were boring but bosses. Or boyfriends. It was a good smile. But it doesn't work anymore. The magic isn't there anymore. Because I just don't care anymore. *(She sits close to EDDIE and attempts a smile. A very tired and sad smile.)* But can you see what a nice smile it used to be? Can you see how nice things used to be? *(ALICE and EDDIE stare at JULIE.)*

ALICE. *(Pause. Softly.)* You have an anchovy stuck on your tooth. *(JULIE just stares at ALICE.)* It might be an olive. I'm not sure. It's just very distracting. *(pointing to her mouth)* It's here. Right back... *(JULIE violently slaps ALICE's arm away.)*

EDDIE. *(sensing trouble)* Hey.

ALICE. *(There is an awkward silence. Near tears.)* Julie. I think we should forget about all this. This whole bad evening. And call it a night.

EDDIE. *(quickly)* Yeah, let's call it a night.

JULIE. *(softly)* I hit you, Alice.

ALICE. It's all right. We'll send Eddie home. You'll take

a Valium and everything will be fine.

EDDIE. *(quickly)* Yeah, send me home.

JULIE. Don't you want to hit me back?

EDDIE. *(to ALICE)* Please, God don't hit her back!

ALICE. *(softly)* It's not nice to hit people. I'll turn the other cheek. *(Rises and moves away from JULIE.)*

JULIE. *(Follows her slowly.)* You always turn the other cheek. *(Moves closer to ALICE.)* They taught us to turn the other cheek.

ALICE. *(scared)* They?

JULIE. Hit me back, Alice. Maybe if we hit back we'll be better people.

ALICE. I'm not gonna hit you.

JULIE. Come on, Alice. *(Shoves ALICE slightly.)*

EDDIE. Hey!

ALICE. I'm not gonna hit you. *(JULIE shoves ALICE harder against the wall.)*

EDDIE. HEY!!! *(Extends his feet and slams them down hard on the coffee table.)* LEAVE HER ALONE!!! *(JULIE stops. She turns slowly and looks back at EDDIE. Pause. EDDIE suddenly takes charge.)* No more rough stuff! No more hitting! Alice, untie me. I'm getting out of here.

ALICE. *(Moves over hurriedly to EDDIE.)* I'm sorry about all this, Eddie. She's really a very nice girl. You should see her in make-up and with heels. She's very nice. *(Starts to untie his hands.)*

EDDIE. *(to JULIE)* You're sick, you know that! You're really pathetic. *(to ALICE)* I'd move out of here as soon as I could. *(back to JULIE)* Nobody gives a shit about your problems. If your life's screwed up that's your problem.

ALICE. *(Struggles with the cord behind EDDIE's back.)* Julie, could you help me? It's all knotted.

EDDIE. You know what your trouble is? You should be married and raising kids. You wouldn't have time to think about how rotten your life is. You wouldn't have time to think at all. You'd be exhausted. But happy!

ALICE. *(to JULIE)* We need scissors.

EDDIE. You're an attractive woman. Pull yourself together and get yourself a husband! *(JULIE heads into the kitchen.)* You girls don't know how good you got things. You could spend the rest of your life sitting on your ass watching "General Hospital."

ALICE. "All My Children." I'd watch "All My Children." *(JULIE comes out of the kitchen with a pair of scissors. She moves over to EDDIE and starts to work on the knotted cord behind his back.)* Nobody's gonna bust your chops if you don't succeed. If you don't have a career. Why knock yourself out? If you can't stand the heat of the real world ... go back to the kitchen! *(Screams in pain.)* AAAA-AAAAAAH!

ALICE. Julie! Be careful! You cut his hand.

EDDIE. Goddamnitt! Stupid Idiot!!!

ALICE. It's all right, Eddie. It's just a flesh wound. Julie, go get the Bactine. *(But JULIE doesn't move. She stares down at EDDIE. The scissors still in her hand.)* Julie?

EDDIE. *(Senses danger.)* Alice.

ALICE. *(Notices the ominous look in JULIE's eyes. Carefully.)* Julie, give me the scissors.

EDDIE. Alice, get those scissors.

ALICE. Julie, please?

EDDIE. Please, Alice. *(JULIE moves in slowly to EDDIE*

and raises the scissors. She touches his throat with them. Pressing them against his flesh.)

ALICE. *(Stares in shock. Softly.)* Oh God.

EDDIE. *(Stares up at JULIE. Petrified with fear. There's a terrifying moment of dangerous silence. Quietly.)* Julie ... Please. *(He clears his throat.)* ... Don't ... *(Clears his throat again.)* ...Don't hurt me ... Please ... I got my whole life ahead of me ... don't take it away from me ... Don't ... I don't ... I don't wanna die... I don't wanna... (Suddenly; softly EDDIE is crying. He lowers his head and allows the gentle sobs to overcome him. JULIE watches him for a long moment. The scissors still poised at his throat. She reaches out gently and touches the tears on his cheeks. Slowly; silently at first, JULIE begins to cry. Giving in to the tears, she sits slowly on the couch. The scissors go limp in her hand. She and EDDIE sit next to each other on the couch. Crying.)*

ALICE. *(Moves a step closer to them. Watching them as they cry. Touched by the scene. Softly.)* You're crying. Look at you.

JULIE. *(trying to fight it)* Damnitt!

ALICE. Julie?

JULIE. GODAMNITT! *(Slams the scissors down on the coffee table and rises quickly from the couch. She moves over to her purse and searches hurriedly for a small box of Kleenex.)*

ALICE. *(Hurries over to JULIE. Leaving EDDIE, still crying, on the couch.)* Are you OK?

JULIE. *(upset)* NO! I'm crying!

ALICE. *(Puts a comforting arm around JULIE.)* That's all right, Julie. Let it out.

EDDIE. *(softly)* Could I have a Kleenex?

JULIE. *(to ALICE)* It's *not* all right! I'm trying to assert myself! This isn't asserting myself. I wanna be strong!

EDDIE. I need a Kleenex.

ALICE. *(to JULIE)* Holding scissors at the throat of a Pizza Man isn't strength. Trust me.

JULIE. *(sobbing)* Well, it's a beginning!

EDDIE. *(louder)* Kleenex.

ALICE. *(to JULIE)* It's attempted assault, Julie! Attempted assault with pinking shears!

EDDIE. *(Suddenly screams to get their attention.)* HEY!!!!!!

JULIE. *(Whirls around and yells at him.)* Don't yell at us!

EDDIE. *(yelling)* I need a little help here!

JULIE. I don't give a shit what you need! *(JULIE confronts him.)* Look what you did to me! Are you happy? You made me cry! You made me vulnerable!

EDDIE. I didn't do a goddamn thing! I came here to deliver a PIZZA! *(JULIE moves away to pour a stiff drink.)*

ALICE. Would anybody like a Valium?

EDDIE. *(angrily)* Look at me, GODDAMNITT! *(He struggles up from the couch and pursues JULIE.)* Look at what you did to ME! You tied me up! You took advantage of me! Stuck scissors in my throat and told me all your goddamn problems! Tried to *RAPE ME!*

ALICE. *(panicked)* Eddie, please. Keep it down.

EDDIE. I'm a human being! I got my own problems!

JULIE. Back off! Sit down!

EDDIE. *(on a roll)* A wife and a kid to support! A lousy job to do it on! Responsibilities for the rest of my life!

JULIE. *(turning away)* I don't have to listen to this.

EDDIE. *(Follows close behind her.)* House payments! Car

payments! Do you know how many pairs of tennis shoes my kid goes through in a year? Twelve! And who do you think pays for them?

ALICE. You do.

EDDIE. My wife does! She's got a better job than me! She's even got a goddamn retirement fund!!!

JULIE. Good for her!

EDDIE. *(Squares off with her. The two are face to face.)* You're a bitch.

JULIE. You're a prick.

EDDIE. What do you want from me? My balls?!!!

JULIE. In my teeth!

EDDIE. You wanna hurt me, is that it? Is that gonna make things better?! You wanna stick the scissors all the way in next time? Maybe kill me!?

JULIE. *(topping him)* YOU DESERVE TO BE KILLED!!! *(There is a long, awful silence in the room. EDDIE and ALICE stare at JULIE. Shocked.)*

JULIE. *(Speechless. She's stepped over the edge and she knows it. Reality has slapped her in the face. She backs away from EDDIE slowly. Humiliated and terrified, she sets her drink down gently. Quietly.)* What am I saying? ... I don't know what I'm saying anymore. *(She moves away from EDDIE and over to an armchair. She sits exhausted.)* First I want to rape you. And then I want to kill you. For what? For everything that's wrong in my life? It's not your fault. You've got nothing to do with it. *(beat)* They're *my* problems. *My* life. *(softly)* I just want people to stop trying to mold me. Telling me who I am. What I should be. And how to be it. I want to be in control of my life.

EDDIE. *(softly)* So do I. *(JULIE turns and looks over at*

EDDIE.)

ALICE. Everybody wants that, Julie.

JULIE. But I don't know where to start.

ALICE. You already started. *(JULIE looks at ALICE.)* It was your idea to rape Eddie.

EDDIE. Personally. I don't think it was a great start.

ALICE. *(Moves over to JULIE.)* You're the reason he's tied up, Julie. It's your responsibility. You started this. Finish it.

EDDIE. *(getting nervous)* Hold it. Wait a minute...

JULIE. *(to ALICE)* I don't know how to finish it.

EDDIE. *(nervously)* What do you mean "finish it"? What do you mean by that?

ALICE. *(Reaches for the scissors on the coffee table. She holds them out to JULIE. Softly.)* Untie him, Julie. Send him home. *(JULIE looks at the scissors for a moment. A beat, and she takes them from ALICE. She moves over to EDDIE. EDDIE stands frozen. Too terrified to move. JULIE comes up close behind him and with one quick cut releases him from his bondage. EDDIE takes a deep breath and rubs his wrists.)*

JULIE. I'm sorry, Eddie.

EDDIE. *(Looks at her.)* Yeah. Well ... Nobody really got hurt. I guess. *(He clears his throat. ALICE hands him the box of Kleenex. To ALICE.)* No, I'm fine.

ALICE. I wasn't sure.

EDDIE. *(quickly)* Throat's dry. *(JULIE hands EDDIE her full glass of scotch and he belts it down quickly. He hands her back the glass. And the three of them look at each other for an awkward beat.)* Well, I guess that's it, huh? I guess I can go. Right? *(JULIE nods.)*

ALICE. *(Extends her hand quickly to EDDIE.)* It was very

nice meeting you, Eddie. Very, very nice.

EDDIE. *(Shakes ALICE's hand.)* Yeah. Well. I guess I better go. *(He turns and starts for the door. As he opens it, he suddenly hesitates. He looks back at the two women. He steps back into the room.)*

JULIE. What's wrong?

EDDIE. *(Looks at them. Almost too embarrassed to speak.)* I feel close to you guys. I cried in front of you. I shared stuff with you I never told anybody.

JULIE. Really?

EDDIE. Never.

ALICE. *(There's another awkward pause.)* So what's the problem? It sounds like you had a wonderful time.

EDDIE. *(Waits a moment. Embarrassed...)* I just feel ... different.

JULIE. Would you like to stay and talk about it?

ALICE. There's nothing to eat in the house ... But I guess we could call Chicken Delight...

EDDIE. *(quickly)* No, don't call anybody! *(beat)* I'm fine. *(quietly)* I'll live with it. *(He starts out.)*

JULIE. So will I. *(EDDIE stops and looks at JULIE. She holds out her hand; a gesture of peace. An understanding. EDDIE reaches his hand out to her. And then, turning, he exits. JULIE heads over to the bar.)*

ALICE. *(Closes the door behind her. She leans wearily against it.)* God! I thought he'd never leave. I'm exhausted!

JULIE. *(Pours herself a night cap.)* What a shitty thing to do.

ALICE. What?

JULIE. He's such a nice guy. He's so sweet.

ALICE. *(wearily)* Who?

JULIE. *Eddie!*

ALICE. Don't worry about it. He'll probably rush home to his wife and tell her all about it. He'll have a good cry in her arms. And they'll have the best sex of their lives.

JULIE. You think?

ALICE. We probably saved the marriage.

JULIE. I hope so ... I hope something good comes from all this.

ALICE. Me too.

JULIE. But I'm not sure.

ALICE. *(Turns slowly and stares at JULIE.)* You're *not* sure?

JULIE. I still don't know how to fix my life.

ALICE. *(incredulously)* We went through this for *NO-THING?*

JULIE. I know *one* thing.

ALICE. Thank God!

JULIE. I can't go through another night like this.

ALICE. I COULDN'T *LIVE* THROUGH ANOTHER NIGHT LIKE THIS!

JULIE. But I don't know if things are going to get better.

ALICE. *(Suddenly confronts JULIE. She grabs the scotch glass out of her hand. Exploding.)* FIX YOUR LIFE, JULIE! *JUST FIX IT!* I hate people like you. You and Eddie. You're so goddamn wishy washy. You know what your problem is? You had an easy childhood. You had a good couple of years and now you want the rest handed to you on a platter. You're two, spoiled, middle class kids! You should have spent your formative years like I did. In Chubettes!

Something like that gets you ready for the world. *That* and being Jewish.

JULIE. *(sarcastically)* That's my problem? I'm not Jewish?

ALICE. It helps ... It gives me something to hold on to. You want to know what my family's philosophy is?

JULIE. No more life philosophies. *Please.* I had one. And it fucked me up.

ALICE. Well, this one works. It's been around for years. It was passed down from my great-grandfather. An immigrant from Russia. He used to sit us on his knee. Bounce us up and down a couple of times, and tell us... "Life, my child ... is a bitch. And then you die."

JULIE. Your great-grandfather said this?

ALICE. On my mother's side.

JULIE. He said this to little children?

ALICE. In Yiddish. It might lose something in the translation.

JULIE. That's a terrible philosophy to give kids!

ALICE. "Keep smiling" is a healthy one?

JULIE. All right. You have a point.

ALICE. Never expect wonderful things and you'll never be miserable. It makes sense, Julie. It worked for my great-grandfather. He lived to be 94 years old ... and then he was hit by a bus. *(JULIE just looks at ALICE. ALICE explains.)* "Life's a bitch ... And then you die." *(ALICE reaches over and lays her hand on top of JULIE's. Softly.)* You'll smile again, Julie. And when you do it'll mean more. Because you got through this. You're a survivor.

JULIE. *(genuinely)* Thank you.

ALICE. *(shrugs)* Sure. *(rising)* Well, anyway. Personally I think it was a profitable evening. You didn't kill anybody. And I made it through tonight without Jerry.

JULIE. My God. That's right. You did.

ALICE. Jerry was very important to me. I built my life around Jerry. I needed Jerry...

JULIE. *(interrupting)* Alice. Don't start.

ALICE. No, I'm fine. I don't need Jerry. I can do fine without Jerry. I went through this whole evening without even *thinking* about Jerry.

JULIE. Good for you. Mazeltov!

ALICE. *(smiles)* Well, I'm going to take a diuretic and go to bed.

JULIE. Goodnight, Alice.

ALICE. *(exiting)* Goodnight, Jerry. *(ALICE disappears into the bedroom. A beat. And JULIE laughs warmly. Her face is beaming. The smile once again is beautiful.)*

(Curtain.)

THE END

FURNITURE AND PROPERTY LIST

ONSTAGE

LIVING ROOM
>Couch
>Armchair
>Coffee table
>End table
>Lamp
>Cabinet
>Television set
>Wooden matches
>Cigarettes
>Throw pillows
>Afghan
>Framed pictures
>Framed posters
>Ashtrays
>Empty beer cans
>TV Guide
>Beer (half full)
>Contemporary telephone
>Julie's wristwatch
>Stereo
>2 extension cords
>Poster of Mexico
>Beer (unopened)
>Silk flowers
>Porcelain vase
>Wastebasket
>L.A. Kings banner
>Bulletin board
>4 Polaroid photos
>Hallmark Valentine card
>Handkerchief
>Yellow pages
>Area rug
>Small kitchen table
>Two chairs

Bolt on front door
Small foam rubber sculpture that looks heavy

KITCHEN
6-pack beer
Refrigerator
Jug of Spanada wine
Quart of scotch
Trash can
Sink
Counter
Diet soda
Bottle of wine
Scotch glasses
Large porcelain ashtray
Roll of two-inch masking tape
Pair of large scissors
Broom
Dustpan
Break away glasses
Scotch #2

OFFSTAGE

CLOSET
Suitcase
Assortment of clothes

BEDROOM
Dresser
Empty plastic bread wrapper
Assortment of props to be thrown
Jewelry box
Pink plastic vibrator
Portable exercise trampoline
Jeans for Julie

THE OFFICE PLAYS
Two full length plays by Adam Bock

THE RECEPTIONIST
Comedy / 2m., 2f. Interior

At the start of a typical day in the Northeast Office, Beverly deals effortlessly with ringing phones and her colleague's romantic troubles. But the appearance of a charming rep from the Central Office disrupts the friendly routine. And as the true nature of the company's business becomes apparent, The Receptionist raises disquieting, provocative questions about the consequences of complicity with evil.

"...Mr. Bock's poisoned Post-it note of a play."
- New York Times

"Bock's intense initial focus on the routine goes to the heart of *The Receptionist's* pointed, painfully timely allegory... elliptical, provocative play..."
- Time Out New York

THE THUGS
Comedy / 2m, 6f / Interior

The Obie Award winning dark comedy about work, thunder and the mysterious things that are happening on the 9th floor of a big law firm. When a group of temps try to discover the secrets that lurk in the hidden crevices of their workplace, they realize they would rather believe in gossip and rumors than face dangerous realities.

"Bock starts you off giggling, but leaves you with a chill."
- Time Out New York

"... a delightfully paranoid little nightmare that is both more chillingly realistic and pointedly absurd than anything John Grisham ever dreamed up."
- New York Times

SAMUELFRENCH.COM

CPSIA information can be obtained
at www.ICGtesting.com
Printed in the USA
LVHW012112200219
608166LV00017B/656/P